BAD BLOOD

A WITCHES OF CLEOPATRA HILL NOVELLA

CHRISTINE POPE

DARK VALENTINE PRESS

BAD BLOOD

Copyright © 2017 by Christine Pope

ISBN: 978-1-946435-06-4

Published by Dark Valentine Press

Cover design by Lou Harper

Ebook formatting by Indie Author Services

AUTHOR'S NOTE

In several of the Witches of Cleopatra Hill books, there are hints that the ongoing feud between the Wilcox and the McAllister witch clans goes back much further than the attempted kidnapping of Ruby McAllister by Jasper Wilcox in the 1940s.

Here are the true origins of that feud....

1

New York City, April 1877

HANNAH MCALLISTER COULDN'T HELP BUT gawk at the plate-glass magnificence that confronted her. *R.H. Macy's,* proclaimed the sign above the door, while the shop windows offered the promise of all sorts of delights, from lacy parasols to beautifully be-flowered hats. She touched one hand to the straw hat she wore, wondering if it looked obviously homemade compared to the sartorial splendor displayed in the window—and on the streets of the city itself. For this outing, she had worn her best blue dress, but now she thought it must appear terribly plain and drab to anyone with a discerning eye.

"Are ye plannin' to go inside, or are ye just goin' ta look?" her brother Ian teased her.

"Go inside, of course," Hannah replied, lifting her chin. His Highlands accent sounded so loud, so conspicuous. She had spent the two weeks of their passage on the steamer they'd taken from Liverpool listening to the passengers from first class as much as possible, doing her very best to absorb the way they pronounced each word, the way they lifted a teacup or paused to pull a handkerchief from a reticule. It hadn't been easy, but she'd found that if she put on her best gowns and was quiet and smiled her prettiest smiles, the stewards left her alone for the most part. The very last thing she wanted was to be seen as some poor immigrant girl from the Highlands, her Scottish burr proclaiming her origins as soon as she opened her mouth. She was on her way to a new land, and desperately wanted to fit in.

Ian, unfortunately, appeared to lack any similar concerns. His blue eyes glinted at her now, full of laughter at her pretensions. At least he had not told her to leave off with her affectations. No doubt he found her funny more than anything else. But that was Ian. The whole world appeared to divert him, even though there had been precious little amusing about it lately.

Still with her chin in the air, she entered the department store. At once the sights and sounds threatened to overwhelm her. Which way to go? The far side of the shop's ground floor, where she could spy racks and racks of fabric in every shade of the rainbow? The glass case with its tempting display of fine kid gloves and even finer linen handkerchiefs? Or perhaps all the way to the back, where she thought she glimpsed rows of shining boots and delicate-heeled shoes?

So many different goods, all in one place. Certainly there had been nothing like this in their village of Halkirk back in Scotland, or even in Liverpool, from whence she and two dozen of her clan members had set forth to these American shores. When they'd first arrived in Liverpool, Hannah had never thought she would see a city larger or more bustling, more filled with accents and languages from all over the world. However, New York made Liverpool appear as small as the village where she'd been born, with its crowded streets and tall buildings, the vast expanse of Central Park, where she had gone with her brother just this past weekend. In a way, Hannah was glad that the family would not remain here in New York, that they would be striking out for the Arizona Territories just as soon as all the necessary arrangements had been made.

Besides, New York was the province of the Van Horn witches, and they would certainly not be willing to share their territory with a clan of newly arrived witches and warlocks from Scotland. A brief stay such as this one was allowed until further travel arrangements could be made, but nothing more. The telegram from Mrs. Van Horn, the New York clan's *prima,* had made that much painfully obvious.

"I hae na use for girlish fripperies," Ian said. Hannah tried not to wince as several curious glances were sent his way, most notably from a pair of ladies who looked as though they had stepped from the pages of a fashion catalogue, from their elaborately curled hair and perfectly tilted hats to their gowns of elegantly bustled silk and faille. "I'll be up the second floor, inspectin' the leather goods. Ye ken find me there when ye've finished."

"Of course," she replied formally, and her brother shot her another amused grin before ambling off in the direction of the staircase.

Doing her best to ignore the disdainful stares of the well-dressed ladies who stood by a case of beaded and embroidered reticules, Hannah judged it wisest to go toward the back of the store where the yard goods were kept. In her own bag—a much plainer specimen she had tatted herself— she had two precious silver dollars that she'd vowed to spend as wisely as possible. High heels and tortoiseshell combs and purses embroidered with silken flowers were all very well, but they would not do her much good in the wilds of Arizona. Better to see if she could purchase some yardage for a new gown, something lightweight but sturdy. She had heard that the Arizona Territories were hot as fire, although she hoped the tales were mostly exaggeration. The Highlands of Scotland did not provide much preparation for living in those sorts of conditions.

Hannah was happy to see that the clerks at the fabric counter were both occupied with other customers, which meant she would be able to inspect the goods offered there at her leisure, rather than being pressured by a salesclerk to make a decision quickly so she wouldn't waste too much of their precious time.

Still, the assortment offered there was extensive enough to be dizzying…silks and wools and cottons in a bewildering variety of colors and patterns. Something plainer would be more versatile—and, she hoped, less expensive. Because of her bright red hair and green eyes, she tended to choose shades of blue and green, although she still quietly longed for pink, even if several of the women in her family took pains on a regular basis to tell her that it was not a becoming shade for a redhead.

But there was a very nice stripe in deep blue and dark emerald. In her store of trims, now carefully packed away in a steamer trunk, she had some dark blue ribbon that she thought would be a very good match, meaning she wouldn't have to purchase any additional trim to complete the gown. How much per yard, though? She very much feared that the prices here would be far higher than in Thurso, the town closest to the tiny village where the McAllisters lived.

Once lived, she reminded herself, fighting back the wave of sadness that threatened to pass over her. It was all well and good to pretend that this was all a grand adventure, the small McAllister clan starting over in the new world, but the real truth of it was that they'd fought a losing battle to hang on to the lands that had been theirs for nearly a thousand years, until they had no choice but to accept the offer given by their victors, to have every last one of the McAllisters pick up and leave, never to return.

Melancholy didn't have much of a chance to overwhelm her this time, however, for even as she clutched her reticule and told herself that she could not allow such a display of weakness in public, she felt a strange tingle at the base of her spine, the tingle that always signaled she was in the presence of another of her kind. It couldn't be Ian; witches and warlocks used this unspoken warning system to recognize other witch-folk when they were in close enough proximity, but that warning only occurred in the presence of strangers, not around relatives or other people they knew well.

Hannah half-turned, attempting to identify who in the vicinity might be a witch or warlock. Certainly not either of the clerks behind the counter, nor the customers who clustered a few feet from her, inspecting the bolts of fabric the shopgirls had fetched down from the shelves. No, as her gaze moved from one person to the other, she could tell it was none of them.

Then she saw him.

The man had just paused at the far end of the counter, his gaze directed toward the shelves of fabric a few feet away. However, Hannah noticed at once the way his eyes shifted ever so slightly in her direction before returning to the yardage on display. It seemed clear enough to her that he'd been able to tell she was a witch.

And Goddess, he was handsome. A few years older than she, most likely, but still not more than twenty-five at the most. Tall, and with coal-black hair and eyes, coloring made all the more exotic by the large-brimmed hat and sweeping dark coat he wore. Hannah didn't think she'd seen a hat like that ever before, not even on the crowded streets of New York, where one might think it was possible to see almost anything.

Oh, dear, he was coming toward her. Calmly, slowly, as though there was nothing odd about approaching a strange young woman in a public place. Perhaps it wasn't, here in America; Hannah had been here with her fellow exiled clan members for less than a week, but she'd already noticed that things were done very differently in New York. It wasn't merely the way people spoke, or dressed…more how they acted toward one another, how they reacted to various situations. Everything was brisk and fast, even more no-nonsense than a Scottish Highlander.

But then, witches and warlocks had their own rules about certain matters. If one was to encounter a member of a different clan in public, it was considered rude to ignore that person. This stranger must have decided that the etiquette which involved witch-folk was more important than any arbitrary rules about whether it was considered polite to approach a young woman with whom one was not formally acquainted.

He paused a foot or so away from her, and gave a slight bow. "Afternoon, miss," he said. His voice was nicely low, but the words themselves were almost clipped, precise. Hannah had spent enough time studying people's accents that she guessed he must be from here in New York, or at least somewhere in America's northeast. "I couldn't help but notice…." He let his words trail off there, but he didn't need to say anything else. She knew exactly what it was that he had noticed. "May I introduce myself? I'm Nathan Wilcox."

Hannah smiled and extended a gloved hand.

"Hannah McAllister." Although she didn't recognize the warlock's surname, that didn't mean very much. He could still be a member of the Van Horn clan; various last names always crept into the witch families due to marriage with outsiders.

However, because this Nathan Wilcox wasn't wearing gloves, she could tell that he wasn't married, for he had no ring. Or perhaps it was not the custom for men to wear wedding rings here in America. She didn't know for sure, and of course she didn't dare ask.

Besides, what did it matter? She was already spoken for.

"Forgive me, Miss McAllister—are you newly arrived in town? For I don't think I detect much of New York in your voice."

Oh, bother. Had he still heard the burr of her accent, even though she'd done her very best to erase it? A sudden blush bloomed in her cheeks, but she managed to chuckle and say, "You have a good ear, Mr. Wilcox. No, I am not from New York. My family is only staying here for a short time while we arrange travel west."

At those words, a sudden smile lit up his face. Something about that smile sent even more blood rushing to her cheeks. She already thought him handsome, but with a new light in those black eyes, and a flash of his white teeth, he was truly devastating.

No, she should not be thinking of anyone as "devastating." She was already promised to her cousin Boyd, a betrothal arranged by the former *prima* before she'd died trying to defend the clan. True, Boyd was sandy-haired and slight of build and lackluster in every way, but he had been the *prima*'s son, and therefore considered quite a catch. Hannah knew she should have felt honored to be engaged to him, but really, he did seem like a very poor specimen when compared to the handsome warlock who stood before her now.

"That is a coincidence, then," Mr. Wilcox said. "For my family is also here in New York to plan our passage west."

A rush of delight, of anticipation, went through her at that remark, even though she knew she should not allow herself to care where this Nathan Wilcox might be traveling. Still, the thought of another witch clan going to the Arizona Territories made her feel not quite so alone. And that was even more foolish, because it wasn't as though the McAllister contingent consisted only of her and her brother Ian and her Uncle Joseph…and the unfortunate Boyd. No, there were twenty-four of them here now, and more who would follow soon enough. Joseph had thought it wise to come here with a smaller group, head west and get settled as best they could, and then send for the rest of the clan, who were currently lingering in Liverpool until the time came for them to sail to America. The Waterhouse clan held sway in that part of Britain, but their *prima* had graciously allowed the displaced McAllisters to stay there for an extended time, as long as the situation wasn't permanent.

"To the Arizona Territories?" she inquired, then feared the question had sounded entirely too hopeful.

"At first," Nathan Wilcox replied. "We haven't quite decided on our final destination yet. My brother—the head of our clan—has a mind to push on all the way to California, but the northern part of Arizona might be acceptable as well. We have heard that there are none of our clans there, only down in the south, where the de la Paz family has been settled for generations. Luckily, they do not seem inclined to spread northward, which means those lands are open to us."

"Is that so?" Hannah did her best to keep her disappointment from her tone, because there was no real reason to be disappointed, was there? She had only just met this man; they would speak politely, and then he would return to his family and go on with his day, just as she should with hers. Something he had said piqued her curiosity, however. "Your brother is the leader of your clan? Is that very common in America?"

The pleasant smile Nathan had been wearing faded abruptly. His expression guarded, he said, "Not so very common, I think, but it works well enough for us."

Clearly, she had touched a nerve. Hannah could not help but wonder how Mr. Nathan Wilcox's brother had come to lead their clan, for she had not heard of such a thing happening for hundreds and hundreds of years. Once upon a time, men had ruled the witch families, but they were too warlike, too inclined to create conflict where there should be none. Such battles between witch clans attracted far too much attention, and so it came to be that women became the guardians of their families, and the territorial lines strictly observed.

Unfortunately, it was still not a perfect solution, especially in places where the population of the clans grew with each generation, while the land to support them could only remain the same. That was how the McAllisters had been forced out, their *prima* killed by the dastardly doings of the McDougalls. Now the McAllister clan's *prima* was Caitriona, a young woman barely older than Hannah herself. Still grieving the loss of her mother and the only home she'd ever known, and with her own husband a lad quite unready to take any kind of a leadership position, Caitriona allowed her

Uncle Joseph to make most of the important decisions.

How precisely that was different from Nathan Wilcox's brother being the official leader of his clan, Hannah wasn't certain, and yet something seemed to tell her the situations were not the same at all. "That is interesting," she said, since Nathan continued to watch her with that guarded expression, as though waiting for some kind of condemnation on her part. "I suppose I shall have to get used to all sorts of new things here in America."

To her relief, the smile returned. "Oh, yes, I think you shall. Your clan comes from Scotland?"

"Yes." This time, she was the one having difficulty maintaining her smile. So far they had only spoken of the sorts of commonplaces that any two people meeting in public might discuss, and she prayed that he would be discreet enough to keep their conversation on those kinds of topics. It was certainly not wise to discuss anything related to their witch clans while in public—especially a public place as crowded as R.H. Macy's.

He seemed to understand, for he only said, "Then I think you will find it very different here. Have you been to Central Park yet?"

It had been one of the first places she'd visited here in New York, for she had been determined to experience that wonder of the world for herself almost as soon as she and her fellow clan members had settled in the second floor of their boarding house on Stuyvesant Street. She wondered why Mr. Wilcox had asked. "Yes, I went only a few days ago. It is quite splendid, isn't it?"

One corner of his mouth twitched slightly. "Yes, I think so." He paused, then went on, "Would you be at all interested in seeing it again?"

Her breath caught. What a question! She knew she should demur, should tell him that she was quite consumed with family business, and did not know when she would be free to visit the various sights of New York. However, that was a lie, because the truth was that she did not have much to occupy herself at the moment. Uncle Joseph and Aunt Isobel were the ones who seemed to spend every waking moment consulting train timetables and poring over maps, attempting to determine the most economical way to get the contingent of McAllisters to the Arizona Territories. And it was not simply the question of the train, but also the need to procure transport by wagon for the final leg of the journey, for the railroad ended in Pueblo, Colorado, and they would have to go overland after that. All these preparations were being managed with the utmost care, for the clan did not have a great deal of spare cash, only enough to cover the expenses of the journey itself, as well as the purchase of a bit of land once they reached their destination.

And there was also Boyd, plain, plodding Boyd, who had taken the death of his mother in phlegmatic stride, just as he did everything else. If he grieved, he did not give much sign of it. At any rate, Hannah knew that she should politely decline Nathan Wilcox's invitation, tell him she would be honored, but that she was promised to another and so not at liberty to go walking with anyone who was not her betrothed.

But....

She looked up at Nathan, looked at his shining dark eyes, so very different from Boyd's washed-out blue. A few ladies passing by on their way to the notions counter stared at the Wilcox warlock in a way that should have been considered extremely forward...only Hannah knew exactly how they felt. She wanted to stare, too.

In truth, she wanted to do much more than that. The need stirring in her was something of a surprise, for she had never reacted in such a way to a man before. She'd thought that perhaps she simply did not possess the hot blood to match her fiery hair, which, considering her betrothal to her cousin Boyd, could only be a blessing.

Would it be so very bad, to go walking in Central Park with Nathan Wilcox? Surely one could not find a more public place than that. She wanted to learn more about his family, about why they were also headed west. She could...gather information. Like a spy. Yes, that would work very well. Her Uncle Joseph could not give her too much trouble over providing such a valuable service to her clan. And in the meantime, she would be able to spend just a little more time with this fascinating Wilcox warlock.

"That sounds very fine, Mr. Wilcox," Hannah said boldly. "When would you like to go?"

2

NATHAN CHOSE TO WALK TO THE FLAT WHERE the family was staying while here in New York, rather than take a cab or a streetcar. He knew he needed to clear his head before he faced his brother Jeremiah—Jeremiah, whose eyes saw far too much.

The meeting with Hannah McAllister had, of course, not been by mere accident. Although Nathan did not have Jeremiah's talent for bending magic to his will, of shifting it and changing it in a way no one else could, or their brother Samuel's gift of instantly transporting himself from place to place, Nathan's inborn talent for sensing the presence of witches and warlocks at a far greater distance than their usual sense for such things had come in handy in this case. As soon as the McAllister clan had disembarked from their steamer, he'd known that a large group of witches and warlocks had arrived in town, a clan clearly not affiliated with the Van Horns or any of their associated families.

Jeremiah had instructed Nathan to set forth and discover what he could. It had been easy enough to learn that the newly arrived witches and warlocks had taken a flat on Stuyvesant Street, in a neighborhood of modest houses not nearly fine enough for the Van Horns, and yet several steps up from the teeming streets where most new immigrants found themselves. He'd observed their comings and goings for a few days —at a safe distance, of course, one far enough from their lodgings so they couldn't detect his presence—and had determined that, like the Wilcoxes themselves, the McAllisters had been given permission by Eugenia Van Horn, the *prima* of that clan, to stay here in New York while they made their arrangements to travel west. It was a customary sort of courtesy, although Nathan was still mildly shocked that Mrs. Van Horn had allowed the Wilcoxes to do such a thing when they had all but been run out of Connecticut with torches and pitchforks following their break from their Winfield elders and the elevation of Jeremiah to *primus*. The elders from some of the clans here in New York State had participated in that rout, but the Van Horns had held themselves aloof, apparently not wishing to dirty their hands—a command Nathan guessed had come directly from Eugenia Van Horn herself.

That chilly, formidable lady, with her heavy knot of iron-grey hair at the back of her neck and a large hair brooch, encircled with garnets, at the throat of her high-necked black silk gown, had looked at Jeremiah with the expression of someone inspecting a new species of rat that had somehow managed to infiltrate the gloomy splendor of her mansion in Gramercy Park. In the end, though, she had only said, "You have one month to arrange your affairs, Mr. Wilcox. After that, you may assume that you have overstayed your welcome."

Jeremiah, who always appeared the master of every situation in which he found himself, in that moment looked more like a poor relation who was relieved to learn that his pension would not be taken away after all. He had given his thanks, and bowed, and said he would make certain that he and the rest of his family would be gone as soon as was humanly possible.

"I do not know about 'humanly possible,'" Mrs. Van Horn had said in grand tones, "but I would hope that you will manage everything as soon as is magically possible."

The interview had concluded after that, and ever since Jeremiah had been hard at work, securing passage on trains west, expending a good deal of money on telegrams back and forth to Pueblo, Colorado, where they would have to procure wagons and horses for the rest of the journey, and also Santa Fe, where they planned to stop for a few days before continuing on to the Arizona Territories. It was no small matter, for their group consisted of Jeremiah and his wife Lisbeth; Samuel, his wife Grace, and their young son Benjamin; Nathan's brother Edmund and his new bride, Lida; his sister Emma and her husband Aaron; and Jennie Winfield, Nathan's fiancée—not to mention all their luggage and household goods.

At the thought of Jennie, Nathan's mouth turned down slightly. He did not wish to be frowning on this fine spring day, a day that should have been perfect for a walk on New York's streets, and yet he could not quite help himself. The task Jeremiah had given him, of observing the McAllisters, had not seemed like such an onerous one. Not until he met Hannah McAllister, anyway.

Her eyes were green as the new grass in spring, and her hair—it was like a mass of living copper, so rich and burnished that Nathan did not see how any man could look at that hair and not want to bury his face in it so he might breathe it in. Her voice was sweet, just slightly roughened by the Scottish burr she tried so much to hide. Even though he'd learned early on that the McAllisters had come here from Scotland, when he first heard Hannah speak, he was surprised to find she sounded more English than anything else. He had to admit he found it rather charming, that she would think it important to erase any trace of her origins from her accent. It only emerged here and there, and he guessed that most people would not have recognized the slight rolling of her "r"s and the elongated vowels for what they actually were.

In all, he found her most appealing, and had impulsively asked her to go walking with him in Central Park before he'd thought the matter through. Oh, he could probably explain to Jeremiah that it was all part of gathering more information about the McAllisters, who might turn out to be their neighbors if the Wilcoxes did decide to stay in the Arizona Territories, rather than push on to California…but there was Jennie.

The witch clans had a tradition of marrying cousins. Distant cousins in most cases, with judicious additions of nonmagical folk here and there to avoid the danger of inbreeding, so when Jennie had been suggested to him by Jeremiah, Nathan had not thought of refusing the request. It was just the way these things were done, and Jennie, a far-flung Winfield cousin, was certainly pretty enough. Nathan hadn't yet met anyone who could make any claim to his heart, so asking Jennie to marry him had not seemed to be all that great a burden. Much of the time, witches and warlocks recognized the match of their hearts early on, and since he had just passed his twenty-fifth birthday when Jennie's name was brought up, he thought he was one of those who would never find their match, and he might as well marry a suitable cousin.

Now, though....

Hannah McAllister's bright green eyes flashed in his mind again, so different from Jennie's calm brown ones. Right then, Hannah seemed to him a creature of wind and flame, constrained, perhaps, by the heavy blue gown she wore, just as her coppery curls were confined by hair combs and pins, but still with her true nature peeking out nonetheless.

And all that, he told himself, was purest fancy. So she was a lovely young woman. There were many lovely young women in the world, among them his fiancée. He should not be paying any particular attention to Hannah. In fact, he should be thinking of a way to get word to her at her flat on Stuyvesant Street, letting her know that he was most deeply apologetic, but he would not be able to walk out with her tomorrow after all.

However, he knew he would not do such a thing.

When he reached the steps of his own temporary lodgings, Nathan paused to straighten the lapels of the frock coat he wore, and removed his broad-brimmed cowboy hat. Such things, he had been assured, were all the thing out west, although the hat did make him feel rather conspicuous here on New York's busy streets. However, from the way Hannah's eyes had widened in what he assured himself was an admiring fashion as she looked up at him, he guessed his attire had had the desired effect.

His current hesitation stemmed more from a desire to gather himself before he met his brother than to make sure he was sartorially correct. Jeremiah did not miss much…if anything. The moment Nathan opened his mouth and mentioned Hannah McAllister, Jeremiah would be sure to note his brother's interest. Well, he could only do his best. After all, nothing had happened.

Because you were standing in the middle of R.H. Macy's, he told himself. *What if you had been alone in a quiet corner somewhere?*

What will you do when you're alone with her tomorrow?

He attempted to brush that thought aside. "Alone" was a relative term when it came to walking in Central Park. Once again, he and Hannah McAllister would be surrounded by people. True, Central Park offered more opportunities to slip off to a secluded location where they would not be observed, but he would not allow that to happen. He would walk with her, allow himself to admire her, and then escort her home, and so out of his life. After such a short acquaintance, she should leave his thoughts quickly enough.

At least, he hoped that would be the case.

After pulling in a breath, he opened the door to the building and let himself in. Once a large house owned by a single family, it had been broken into flats up and down. The Wilcox contingent occupied the entire second floor, while the first had been taken by a Swedish family with no English. They seemed pleasant enough, and smiled and nodded their blond heads whenever they encountered one of the witches or warlocks from upstairs, but that was the extent of their interactions.

Nathan might once have called that a lucky coincidence, but he'd learned long ago that such things as coincidences did not usually apply to his brother.

After climbing the stairs, Nathan went immediately to his right, to the front sitting room where Jeremiah generally spent his afternoons. It was the space farthest away from the bedroom that Jeremiah's wife Lisbeth occupied—an arrangement that also had not occurred by chance.

The door stood open, so Nathan went in without knocking. Jeremiah sat at a writing desk placed up against the opposite wall, pen scratching away as he pored over a railway timetable and made copious notes. He did not look up as he said, "Ah, Nathan."

How Jeremiah had known it was him, rather than Edmund or Samuel, or even Emma's husband Aaron, Nathan didn't know for sure. Just another of Jeremiah's prodigious gifts, the ones that had led him to break with the Winfield clan, to decide that he must be the one to lead his own little family, rather than submit to the whims of a *prima.*

"Jeremiah," Nathan returned, his tone neutral. He went ahead and took a seat on the settee in the middle of the room, knowing that his brother would attend to him just as soon as he was done with his current batch of notes. On the little table in front of the settee was a teapot and a pair of cups. Although tea was not his favorite libation, Nathan went ahead and poured himself some, thinking that he might as well do something to occupy himself while he was waiting. The tea was now just a little more than lukewarm, but still fragrant enough. Emma's doing, he guessed; certainly his sister-in-law Lisbeth was not the type to lift a finger to help anyone but herself, and Grace would be busy with the new baby —no doubt assisted by Lida and Jennie.

After a minute or two, Jeremiah pushed the papers away and got up from the desk where he'd been sitting. However, he did not seem inclined to take a new seat on the settee, but instead reached down and picked up the remaining teacup from the table and filled it halfway with lukewarm tea. Being Jeremiah, he did not bother with preambles.

"What did you learn?"

"That the McAllisters are only temporary visitors here, as we are. They are headed to the Arizona Territories, although Miss McAllister did not give me any more details than that."

"Miss McAllister?" Jeremiah raised one heavy eyebrow. "So you spoke with her."

"Yes. She recognized that I was a warlock, so we exchanged a few words."

"And she was alone?"

"Not precisely. A young man accompanied her, but he went upstairs while she was looking at the fabric selections. Because he had red hair in almost the same shade as hers, I assumed he was her brother."

"But he didn't see you."

"No. He had not reappeared before I made my goodbyes to Miss McAllister and went on my way." And thank God for that. Nathan had no desire to explain his presence to a protective older brother. At least, he guessed the young man who had disappeared to the upper level of R.H. Macy's was older than Hannah. He was a tall, sturdy-looking fellow, probably not much younger than Nathan himself, while Hannah appeared to be little more than twenty, if even that.

"Another witch clan in Arizona," Jeremiah said, his tone musing. "I am not sure I like the sound of that."

"It's a big place."

"But is it big enough?" He pushed a lock of heavy black hair—the same hair all the Wilcox brothers shared—off his forehead and frowned.

"I should think so. There are not that many of them, as far as I can tell. No more than two dozen at the most."

"Only twenty-four of them here in New York," Jeremiah said. "I have no doubt that there are more in Britain, just waiting for the signal to leave."

"How can you know that?"

"Because it is what I would have done—to come to a new place with only part of the clan, until I was certain of the reception we received." He went to the window and looked outside, although Nathan was not quite sure what his brother might be looking for. Nathan's gift told him that the only people of witch-kind in a quarter-mile radius were those in this very flat. Jeremiah went on, his tone musing, "I wonder why they are here."

"For much the same reason we are, I suppose," Nathan said. "Because we can no longer stay where we came from. No doubt they came out on the wrong side of a clan battle."

"We were not on the wrong side," Jeremiah retorted. "We were outnumbered. That is all."

Would they have prevailed, if there had been more involved in that fight than the Wilcox brothers? Perhaps in the old country, witches fought alongside warlocks, but that was not how things were done in America. Besides, Nathan didn't think any of the women in the family could have helped all that much. His sister Emma was a noted healer, but her gifts were suited for the aftermath of a battle, not to be in the thick of it. Lisbeth, Jeremiah's wife, was quite handy with illusions, which might have been helpful—if she was the type to be helpful at all. Most of the time she complained of headaches, and stayed in bed with her bottle of laudanum. Whenever Nathan was inclined to become impatient with his brother, with his occasionally heavy-handed ways, he thought of how Jeremiah had to endure such a stone around his neck, and kept quiet.

As for Lida and Grace and Jennie—well,

Grace had a newborn to manage, and Lida's talent for speaking with the dead wasn't of much use in the heat of battle. Jennie could call flame to her, which was a more battle-worthy skill. However, since she was a Winfield, she would have been forced to fight her own cousins. Nathan couldn't have asked that of her. It was enough that she had chosen to stay with him, rather than return to her own people.

The memory of that loyalty made him feel even more ashamed of the way he had reacted to Hannah McAllister. Yes, sometimes physical attractions were utterly perplexing, and difficult to control, but he knew he should dismiss that attraction, lest it get him into trouble.

And, he thought, *you had best stop thinking about Hannah at all, unless you want your brother to start asking questions you do not wish to answer.*

"It is better this way," Nathan said, not directly replying to Jeremiah's comment. "We can start over in a new territory, one you can shape how you like. Even if the Winfields and the other New England clans had allowed us to remain, would you really have wanted to continue with all of them always looking over your shoulder, trying to interfere?"

"I suppose not." Jeremiah stepped away from the window and retrieved his teacup, then drained its contents in one swallow. He did not put down the cup, however, but continued to hold it, forefinger tapping against the fine porcelain. One of Emma's cups, Nathan realized, from the rose-painted set that had been a wedding gift. Even then, Jeremiah had been experimenting with his magic in secret, keeping his intentions for creating a new clan hidden from everyone except his three brothers. It wasn't until after Aaron married Emma that Jeremiah had been at all forthcoming. A lesser man might have tried to leave. Aaron, however, pledged his loyalty to his new brother-in-law, and said he was honored to be a part of the new Wilcox clan.

A good man, Aaron.

"You are planning to see her again?" Jeremiah asked then, and Nathan had to keep himself from starting. And here he thought he had done his best to keep his brother from guessing at his plans.

Still, he knew better than to lie. Even younger brothers were not allowed much leeway in the Wilcox family. "Yes," Nathan said, hoping he sounded casual, and not at all invested in this next meeting with Hannah McAllister. "We are going to meet in Central Park at the carousel at four o'clock."

"An innocuous destination, to be sure," Jeremiah responded in equally neutral tones, although something about the sudden glint in his black eyes told Nathan that his brother had all too clear a notion as to how much that particular event was anticipated.

"I thought so. At any rate, I hope to hear more about her clan during that meeting. At the very least, it would be good to know where they plan to settle, so we can make sure to stake our own claim at a safe distance."

"Surely you don't think we Wilcoxes have anything to fear from the McAllisters." One side of Jeremiah's mouth lifted slightly, but that cold glitter remained in his dark eyes. He did not like to be reminded that he hadn't always come out the victor in encounters with other witches and warlocks.

"'Fear' is a strong word," Nathan responded mildly. "I don't get the sense that they have anyone terribly powerful with them. Of course, there are more of them than there are of us, even in the smaller group that's here in New York now. But that isn't what I meant. If the Arizona Territories are as large as we hear they are, then there should be no problem with finding suitable lands, ones that are also conveniently far enough away from the McAllisters that there won't be any reason to come into conflict."

"If we stay there at all. I haven't quite made up my mind."

Up until this point, Nathan had been neutral

on the topic of whether they should make California their final destination, or whether it would be better to remain in Arizona. Now, though, he couldn't help but give voice to one of his misgivings. "I thought there were already witch clans in California," he said carefully.

One of Jeremiah's eyebrows lifted. "There are. But there should be room for all of us in a state that large. It would be no different from settling in the Arizona Territories."

Possibly. The Santiago clan, which had lived in the southern part of California since the time of the first Spanish settlers in the area, probably wasn't all that different from the de la Paz family of southern Arizona when it came to size and strength and influence. Jeremiah already knew he had to steer clear of the Santiagos, due to their overly territorial nature, so Nathan didn't bother to comment. He knew less about the witch clan in the region around San Francisco, but they also sounded well-established. That was why northern Arizona made more sense. The de la Pazes did not range into that area, and no other witch clans had been established there. Even with the McAllisters moving into that part of the territory, there wouldn't be anyone settled there long enough to be too possessive of the lands they'd taken as their own.

However, since that was Jeremiah's judgment

to make, Nathan refrained from arguing. He merely lifted his shoulders and said, "I suppose you are right," then excused himself to go see Jennie. While at R.H. Macy's, he had bought her a packet of pins and some thread.

A peace offering? Perhaps.

He didn't want to admit to himself that he had done nothing which would require such a gift.

Nothing yet, anyway.

3

Hannah did her best to make it seem as if she wasn't overly fussing with her hat, but it was difficult. She wanted to make sure that it was tilted at exactly the right angle so the green feathers that trimmed it would bob gracefully as she walked, rather than sticking out in all directions. True, all it would require was one stiff breeze to ruin the effect, but she had to hope for the best. The day outside seemed placid enough, the fresh green leaves barely shimmering on their branches. She could not have asked for better weather, even if she was one of those lucky witches or warlocks whose gift it was to control the clouds and the rain.

If anyone was curious as to why she had put on her second-best gown on what otherwise should have been an utterly prosaic Wednesday afternoon, none of her family members seemed to give any indication of it. Luckily, Uncle Joseph had gone and taken her cousin Boyd with him—something about procuring more trunks to store the supplies they'd been purchasing here in New York—and Joseph's wife Isobel, who one would have thought was too old for such things, was doing her best to manage the nausea and megrims of early pregnancy. Their daughter Mary was also in a similar state, and so the two of them were more or less confined to the flat, content to have others run errands for them.

Which Hannah was all too happy to do. She in fact had a list of items they required, and would take it with her when she went to meet Nathan Wilcox. Attempting to purchase those sundries while still allowing herself adequate time with the Wilcox warlock might be difficult, but she thought she was up to the task. Ian had gone with Boyd and Uncle Joseph, so he wouldn't be around to ask any awkward questions.

All in all, her family had made this particular outing much easier than she had feared. Thank the Goddess that it was now 1877 and the modern age, and so no one should blink an eye at a young woman going about on her own. She had a few pennies in her reticule for the street car, and had borrowed her Cousin Mary's parasol. In a pinch, it would do well enough to fend off anyone who was inclined to crowd her. Not for the first time, Hannah wished her own particular talent was something a little flashier, something she could use to protect herself. Not that healing wasn't useful, but….

"I shan't be long," she called out to her Aunt Isobel and Cousin Mary, and sailed out the door before they could ask any questions, or even respond to say goodbye.

Hannah allowed herself a sigh of relief as she all but skipped down the front steps, then told herself she needed to appear a little more staid and subdued. After all, going on such prosaic errands as visiting the drugstore or Woolworth's— although even those mundane destinations seemed exotic enough to her—in general did not elicit quite that much of a reaction. She assumed a more sedate pace as she walked to the corner, then headed down toward Broadway so she could get on the streetcar. Good thing she had already made this trip once before, so she knew well enough how to get to Central Park without having to stop and ask for directions.

The streetcar was about half full. Hannah took a seat somewhere in the middle, carefully away from any of the other passengers, and made an effort to keep her gaze fixed on the streets passing by outside. That way, she could avoid making eye contact with anyone. She did not want anyone to approach her. This was a strategy she'd seen other ladies walking alone employ successfully, so she assumed it must work.

To her relief, the ride was uneventful. She alighted at the stop at Broadway and 58th Street, then paused to get her bearings. The carousel was located at the far end of the park, and so she still had something of a walk to get there. Compared to the distance she used to have to travel on foot to get to the nearest town, however, this little stroll was nothing. Besides, the weather was mild and fine, with just enough of a breeze to set the trees rustling and to blow away some of the pall of coal smoke which seemed to be settled perpetually over the city.

Even though it was a time of day when many should be at work, still the walkways were crowded enough, with children rolling hoops along, or lovers walking arm in arm. Hannah wished she might walk like that with Nathan Wilcox, although she doubted she could be that brave. The odds of anyone she knew seeing her were vanishingly small, and yet she knew she couldn't take that risk. No, she would meet with him, and talk with him, and allow herself to bask in his presence...and nothing more. A bit of a harmless flirtation, something she could tuck away and bring out to cherish when life with her Cousin Boyd seemed too pallid and dull.

Flashes of bright color and squeals of excited laughter told her she was drawing near to the carousel. And there it was, painted horses going 'round and 'round, mirrors reflecting the sun with sudden, sharp glints, gold leaf gleaming to rival that sun. Hannah paused in the shade of an elm tree and watched the carousel for a moment, then let her gaze drift around the crowd so she might see if Nathan was there.

She didn't spy anyone in a black hat and a black frock coat, and had to fight back a stab of disappointment. But perhaps she was early. She didn't own a pocket watch, and so she had no clear idea of what time it was. When she left the flat, the clock in the hallway there had told her it was not quite half past two, and so she thought she had given herself plenty of time. For all she knew, Nathan had his own stories to cook up for his family to explain where he might be going, and that could have delayed him as well.

As she looked back toward the carousel, however, her breath caught. For there he was, approaching from the other side of the park, black coat flapping in the breeze, his tall form so handsome, so distinctive, that other women half-turned to watch him pass, even though such evidence of obvious interest was considered quite ill-mannered.

And now he was coming toward her, hat

immediately in hand as he bowed slightly. His coal-black hair shone in the sun, and his dark eyes warmed as he looked at her.

"Afternoon, Miss McAllister."

Oh, how she wished they could dispense with such formalities! But they were barely acquainted, and so addressing one another by their first names was certainly not something either of them would dare to do.

At least…not yet.

"Mr. Wilcox," she said, glad that her voice sounded steady enough.

"I hope you have not been waiting long."

"Oh, no. The streetcar dropped me off not ten minutes ago."

His dark brows drew together. He looked quite formidable when he frowned like that, although it seemed clear enough that he was worried, not angry. "A young lady such as yourself, riding the streetcar alone?"

She gave a negligent lift of her shoulders. "It was nothing, truly. Besides," she went on ingenuously, "my family is in no position to pay for frivolities like private cabs, not when we must save every penny for our trip west."

"It is an expensive undertaking," he agreed, the frown disappearing. "So I suppose I can't fault you for that. Do you know yet when your family plans to leave?"

That was a prospect she didn't much wish to contemplate, although Hannah knew that wishing something away was rarely effective. "The end of next week, I think," she replied. Only a few days ago she had been hoping the journey would begin sooner, for she did not much care for New York, despite its many attractions. It seemed so vast, and so crowded, and on dull, dank days, the very air hurt to breathe. Not today, of course. Today, the sky was so blue that she thought she might have imagined how dark and soot-shrouded the city usually was.

And now she hoped her family would never leave for Arizona, because that meant she would never again see the man who stood before her now.

It seemed that he had noted the lack of enthusiasm in her tone, because he said, "Surely you must be excited to explore a new part of this country."

Hannah summoned a smile and put it on. "Oh, yes, I am. Of course. It will be quite the adventure."

Did those words sound as unenthusiastic to Nathan Wilcox as they did to her? She wished she had only said yes and left it at that.

But there he was, smiling back at her and saying, "It will be very different from Scotland, that is for certain." He paused, and glanced around them, at the laughing children on the carousel, at the mothers and nannies who stood by and watched. "Perhaps you would like to walk someplace where it is a bit quieter?"

Oh, wouldn't she. Quite possibly it wouldn't be thought proper to go off with him to a more isolated section of the park, but right then, she didn't much care. "That sounds like a very good idea."

He offered her his arm, and, after a brief hesitation, she went ahead and took it. There didn't necessarily have to be anything romantic about walking arm in arm with a man; it could be seen as a gesture of courtesy, to make sure that she didn't stumble. Of course, her boots were low-heeled and very sensible, and the gravel walkways carefully groomed, but still....

They left the calliope music of the carousel and the laughing children and the gossiping mothers behind them, and ventured down a path less trodden, one which had carefully planted trees overhanging it, providing some much-needed shade on this bright day. The breeze felt cooler here, and carried with it the scent of warm grass. She could almost pretend she was back in the country, far away from the noise and traffic of New York.

"And how long does your own family plan to stay here in the city, Mr. Wilcox?" she asked.

"Not much longer, either," he said. "We'll want to be across the desert before the full heat of the summer sets in."

Yes, that would be wise. Hannah confessed to herself that she found it difficult to picture the very idea of a desert, of uncounted miles stretching in every direction with only sand and rock and those odd-looking plants called cacti to break up the monotony. She felt quite certain she would not care for it at all, and yet that was where her Uncle Joseph planned to take her—even though he had assured everyone in the family that the high desert of Arizona was not exactly the same as the windswept Sahara, at least according to the accounts he had read.

"I suppose if you're traveling to California, you will have much farther to go."

"If we go to California. It's not settled yet."

Once again she found herself fiercely hoping that the Wilcox clan would get to Arizona and then decide to travel no further. But no, wouldn't that be worse, to know that Nathan Wilcox was so close, and yet might as well have been on the moon? Better he was in California. As her Aunt Mary liked to say, out of sight, out of mind.

Hannah didn't know if she truly believed that. Goddess knows that Mr. Wilcox had been preying on her thoughts ever since she'd met him, whether or not he was physically near her or not.

Perhaps sensing the tumult of her thoughts, he asked, "Do you know where in Arizona you are headed?"

Somehow she managed to smile, and slant a sideways look up at him. "Goodness, Mr. Wilcox. Do you always ask so many questions?"

At once his expression sobered, and he said quickly, "I didn't mean to offend you, Miss McAllister. Please forgive me if you thought I was prying."

She shook her head. "No, I didn't think that at all. It's—well, I suppose the more I talk about it, the more real the whole thing becomes." A bench placed conveniently under a tree caught her eye, and she went on, "Do you mind if we sit for a while?"

"Of course. It does look cool and shady over there."

His hand steady on her arm, he guided her across the grass and over to the bench. She really didn't need his help, not when she was used to running across the hummocky land that surrounded the McAllisters' village back in Scotland, but she liked the pressure of his fingers on her arm too much to pull away. Besides, once they had both sat down, he no longer had a reason to hold her, and so she might as well enjoy his touch while she could.

They seated themselves, and she set her

parasol down and arranged her voluminous skirts as best she could. Good thing she had practiced walking in these gowns while she was on board ship, or no doubt she would have made a fool of herself—tripping over her train, or squashing her bustle by sitting on it directly, rather than discreetly hiking it out of the way before she sat. The simple skirts and blouses from her old life in Scotland were a good deal easier to manage, but she couldn't deny that these gowns, with their tightly laced waists and gracefully draped skirts, were far more becoming.

Overhead, a house finch trilled away. This bench was located somewhat off the path, and so she felt very alone here with Nathan, very far away from anyone else. She was acutely conscious of him sitting on the bench next to her, of how very large and male he seemed. Strange how he should feel so much bigger now that he was sitting at her side, when in reality, the difference in their heights was far more pronounced when the two of them were both standing.

The silence felt all too awkward. Thinking it best to pick up the thread of their former conversation, she said, "As to where we are going, Mr. Wilcox, it is a small town some distance from Prescott, called Jerome. A copper mining town, my uncle tells me."

"Is your clan going into the mining business, Miss. McAllister?"

Nathan Wilcox's dark eyes felt far too intense. A flush touching her cheeks, Hannah replied, "No, I don't think so. But my uncle says that there is a good living to be made from supporting the mining industry. He has it in mind to open a store there, already has a plot of land picked out. And also, he believes that because there are so many people coming and going in such places, and so much activity, that it is less likely anyone will notice...well...you know."

"Notice that you're witches and warlocks, you mean."

She cast a worried glance around as those words left Nathan's mouth, but of course there was no one in the vicinity to hear them. "Yes, that. It's difficult to begin in a new place. We know we must guard what we are, and it seems that such a task will be easier in a town like Jerome."

"No, that makes perfect sense." He paused and looked off in the distance, as though to make sure no one would come walking down the path at the wrong moment. "Forgive me, Miss McAllister—you speak of your uncle, and it sounds as though he is the one in charge. Don't you have a *prima* to make such decisions?"

Hannah's mouth suddenly felt dry. "Yes, we

do, but…." Part of her was telling her to leave it alone, to give him some convenient lie. The truth would only reveal to the Wilcoxes how very weak the McAllisters actually were. But she didn't want to lie to Nathan. How could she lie, with those dark eyes watching her with true sympathy, as though he had already guessed that she was attempting to hide some sort of tragedy from him. "We are here because we were driven out of our home in Scotland. Our *prima* was killed, and her daughter now leads our clan. However, she is still struck by grief, and allows her uncle to make most of the decisions for the clan."

"'Her uncle," Nathan said, his tone musing. "And he is your uncle as well?"

"Yes. Uncle Joseph and my late Aunt Ellen were twins. My mother was their younger sister."

"Was?"

"She died not long after I was born. I scarcely remember her."

The sympathy in Nathan's eyes only deepened. In fact, those eyes were so deep and dark, Hannah thought she might drown in them. She blinked, breaking the contact, and looked away.

"You had no healer?"

"We did, but she could not save my mother. 'Twas said she died of a broken heart as much as anything, for my father had died some months earlier, murdered by one of the McDougalls."

That comment made Nathan Wilcox's dark eyebrows lift in surprise. "Murdered?"

"Oh, yes," Hannah said. No need to keep the bitterness from her tone, not when she knew the handsome warlock sitting next to her could see it clearly on her face. "We have a bloody history, we McAllisters and McDougalls. That is why we are here, you see. They finally succeeded in driving us out."

"I am very sorry."

She lifted her shoulders. A poor response, in the face of so much death, but Hannah had become inured to it. The feud between the two clans had always been a part of her life, something as much a part of the natural order of things as the sun rising in the east and setting in the west.

"It happened. It's done. And now we're here in the new world, and determined to make the best of it."

His hand moved to cover hers. So warm and strong. She shouldn't have been able to feel that much through the crocheted net of her glove, and yet she did, could somehow sense the comfort and strength flowing from him. There was so much she didn't know about Nathan Wilcox, but she did know one thing.

He was good.

She half-turned on the bench. There he was, watching her gravely. Every detail about him seemed so sharp and clear—the sooty fringe of lashes around his eyes, the faintest hint of dark stubble on his cheeks and chin, the tiny cleft in that chin. And yes, the shape of his mouth, not terribly full but so perfectly chiseled, wide and sensual.

No, she couldn't be staring at his mouth. And yet…she was.

Just as he was staring at hers. Once again she could feel herself flush under that regard, as though he was trying to commit every one of her features to memory. In that moment, she knew he must feel it, too, must hate the thought that very soon they would both go their own way and never see one another again.

"I shouldn't…." he began, then stopped.

Shouldn't what? Look at her like this? Sit this close? Or simply be alone in such a way, with everyone in this enormous park occupied with their own business somewhere else?

All questions fled after that, however, because he had leaned in and touched his lips to hers, his mouth so soft yet strong, so impossibly alive. His hands moved to cup her face, tender, touching her so lightly, as if she were made of the finest porcelain, and would shatter from too much pressure.

No one had ever kissed her before. Well, except in the perfunctory way Boyd had pressed his mouth against hers to seal the deal on their betrothal. She had been seventeen, and his touch had elicited no particular reaction, except that she wished to have a long gulp of cider afterward, as if to erase his flavor from her lips.

This, though—this was so very, very different. Her entire body seemed to thrum with a new kind of life, a different kind of sensation. She forgot about the stays compressing her waist, or the heavy bulk of her skirts, or the way the sun beat down on the thick linen of the close-fitting bodice. All she could feel was her blood running in her veins, like warm, delicious fire. And something more, a throbbing in that part of her that she knew she was supposed to ignore, at least until she was a properly married woman.

No wonder. The McAllisters still worshipped the Goddess, and the pantheon that surrounded her, older than the very hills and moors themselves, but they knew how to conduct themselves so they would not attract the attention of their strict Calvinist neighbors. A woman must remain chaste until bound to her husband, and if the men were not quite so circumspect, well, they were still discreet.

Nathan lifted his mouth from hers and gave a quick glance around, as though he expected to see a contingent of her relatives approaching, ready to defend her sullied honor. However, the two of them were still quite alone, their only company the finch in the tree above their head, who seemed to have acquired a partner, for they were now sharing a vociferous exchange of trills.

"I—I beg your pardon," he said, although the heat in his eyes belied the polite words.

"There is no need for you to be sorry," she told him. It was only the truth. Even if he never kissed her again, at least she would have this one memory. She would forever know what a real kiss was supposed to feel like.

"But I took an advantage—"

She tilted her head to one side, considering him. He did look genuinely contrite. Still, she thought she needed to set the record straight. "Nathan Wilcox, I am a witch of the McAllister clan. Do you really think I would have allowed that kiss to continue if I didn't truly want it?"

A reluctant smile tugged at his mouth. "No, I suppose you wouldn't."

"Then let us not have any nonsense about 'taking advantage.'"

He didn't nod, but continued to watch her, even as his smile faded. "But I fear I have not been entirely truthful with you."

"Truthful?" she asked. Thank the Goddess, her voice sounded steady and calm, even though his words awoke a sudden cold fear somewhere deep within her.

A long pause. His jaw tightened, and he said

nothing more. Hannah sat very still, knowing she shouldn't press him, but wishing more than anything that he would tell her what preyed on his mind, no matter how bad it might be.

At last he let out a gust of a breath. "I am engaged to be married."

She didn't know why those words should feel like a blow to the stomach. And she told herself that she was a hypocrite for feeling so stricken, for she was not free to kiss any man except Boyd, and she had just done so.

"So am I," she said, and Nathan's entire body seemed to stiffen. He did not exactly draw away from her, but he might as well have.

"A cousin?" he asked, and she nodded.

"You as well?" she said.

"Yes."

He seemed to have little inclination to say anything after that. Perhaps it was just as well. Perhaps this was where they should leave things. Surely they could be forgiven for this one indiscretion.

But somehow she realized she couldn't do that.

"I don't love him," she said. "It was arranged, as these things often are."

Nathan's mouth twisted. Clearly, this revelation did not come as a relief to him.

Since he did not seem inclined to speak, she went on, "Do you love her?"

Another long silence. He glanced away from her, at the shimmer of sunlight on the trees that surrounded them, at the far-off figures of people taking their oblivious promenades on other pathways throughout the park. Still no one had disturbed them here; Hannah wondered if that was just happy circumstance, or whether Nathan possessed the subtle gift of enforcing isolation when he required it.

At last he said, "No. I like her very much, but that is not the same as love." A pause, and his gaze returned to her, those dark eyes fixed on her face, as though he needed to memorize every detail. "It is not the same as desire."

Warmth flooded her cheeks. Perhaps that was all which existed between them—a physical attraction, the sort of need she'd always been warned against. Surely it couldn't be love, not after they'd barely shared an hour or so together. She'd always wondered how people in books and plays could find themselves so hopelessly, madly in love when they barely knew one another.

Well, now she knew. Because if this was not love, it was certainly a very good counterfeit of that troublesome emotion.

She should get up and walk away now. Not because what Nathan had just revealed offended her, but because she knew if she stayed, she would be setting both of them on a very dangerous course.

And yet…it was as if some sort of irresistible force kept her sitting on that bench, prevented her from doing anything except stare back at him. What should she do? Tell him this had all been a mistake, wish him the best of luck, and then go.

Yet, she stayed.

He reached out and took her hands in his. "Hannah, what do you want? For I will leave, if you tell me to."

Did she want him to leave? No, she thought not. Actually, the very thought of him getting up from this bench and walking away, leaving her forever, was enough to make her heart clench.

"I don't know what I want, Nathan," she whispered. "I only know that I cannot bear the notion of seeing you go away. I am mad—I know that. *This* is mad. Chance brought us together, but I shouldn't allow it to rule me now."

His fingers tightened on hers, pressing the crochet mesh into her skin. She didn't protest, however. Better to have him cling to her more tightly than to not touch her at all. "It wasn't chance," he said. "I sensed the arrival of your family. That's my gift—to be able to detect those with witch blood at a far greater range than what is considered usual. My brother asked me to investigate. That was how I met you."

So much for being like the star-crossed lovers she'd read about in fairy tales. Hannah supposed she should be glad Nathan had been so honest, and yet in that moment she couldn't quite quell the rage which flared within her. She snatched her hands from his grasp, and rose to her feet. "So it had nothing to do with me at all, did it? You knew there was another witch clan here in the city, and so you contrived a meeting to learn more. That was all."

"No—" he began.

She would not listen, though. After all, hadn't he just provided her with the perfect excuse for breaking this off before it could go any further? "Well, I hope I have provided you with enough information to keep your clan happy. I know for myself that I will be well content if you don't come within a hundred miles of Jerome!"

Before he could say anything else, attempt to defend himself, she flounced off, her cheeks burning with righteous rage. Now she could go back to the flat and pretend none of this had ever happened. In less than a week, she would be gone with the rest of her family.

And as for Nathan Wilcox?

She hoped she would never see him again.

4

NATHAN KNEW BETTER THAN TO STOP HER. Heart sick and sore, he watched Hannah go, her slim figure stiff with rage, her trained skirts of patterned green linen twitching with every step.

Truly, wasn't this all for the best?

His body didn't think so. Even as he stared after her until she had disappeared around a bend, it took all his will to force him to remain seated, to not launch himself from that bench and run after her, take her hand and turn her around, kiss her until she forgave him.

He did none of those things, however. Fingers curled around the wooden slats of the bench's seat, he remained where he was until he knew that Hannah McAllister was long gone. At last he stood, feeling as stiff and cramped as a grandfather of eighty years, rather than the man of twenty-five he knew he actually was.

That could have gone better. But because he had not wished to lie to her, he had allowed the truth to separate them, rather than the opposite.

Did it matter, though? What possible end could this come to? He was promised to another, and so was Hannah. True, an engagement was not as difficult to break as a marriage, but still. In this, Hannah had far more to lose than he did. She was engaged to the son of the former *prima,* while Nathan himself was only promised to a distant cousin. Although he disliked the idea of doing so, he knew he still had the option of sending Jennie back to her Winfield relations. No doubt they would be happy to take her in, would be pleased to know that she had renounced her connection to the dastardly Wilcoxes, whereas Hannah's relatives could only see her repudiation of her betrothed as a rejection of the family as a whole.

Damn.

Nathan got up from the bench and walked over to the path, then headed off in the opposite direction from whence Hannah had disappeared. He tried to tell himself it was all for the best. Even if both their clans did end up in northern Arizona, the chances of encountering her would still be exceedingly slim. Although Jeremiah hadn't yet committed to a final destination, he had spoken once or twice of Flagstaff, saying that the town was beginning to boom, and that the vast forests which surrounded the settlement provided ample resources for creating a prosperous lumber business. How far was Jerome from Flagstaff? Nathan couldn't say for sure, although he thought it had to be at least fifty miles based on the maps he'd seen, probably more. And not the civilized miles of the East Coast, with neatly paved roads and carefully placed mile markers, but miles that spanned steep hills and acre upon acre of virgin forest, unmarred by roads or paths.

This thought should have cheered him. Instead, it only made him feel more desolate.

Fists jammed in his pockets, he made his way from the depths of the park to one of the streets that bordered it. However, he did not hail a cab, and there was no way in the world he would avail himself of a streetcar, not when it appeared to him that streetcars were Hannah's preferred mode of transportation. Instead, he walked all the way back to West 147th Street, where he let himself in the front entrance and prayed that no one would be around to spy his return.

Unfortunately, almost as soon as he had ascended the stairs, one of the doors along the center hallway opened. Jennie peered out, began to smile when she saw it was him…and then abruptly went sober as she appeared to get a good look at his face.

"Goodness, Nathan," she said. "Whatever is the matter?"

At once he tried to shift his features into a more placid arrangement. "Oh, nothing at all," he replied, mentally cursing himself for not taking more care to guard his expression before he entered the flat. "I suppose I am just wishing to be gone from this place. Large cities never did agree with me."

This reply seemed to reassure her somewhat, because the smile returned, albeit a little less bright than it first had been, and her dark eyes still appeared somewhat worried. "I can understand that. I think we will all do better once we are on the road. Has Jeremiah said anything of when he wishes to depart?"

"Not yet. Soon, though. He's still setting up the arrangements for the overland portion of our journey. The railway accommodations are a simple enough matter, but trying to manage the logistics of hiring enough coaches to transport all of us is far more difficult. And Jeremiah is also attempting to make contact with the witch clan in Santa Fe, just so we don't come as a complete surprise when we show up on their doorstep to purchase whatever we might need for the last leg of our journey."

"Santa Fe," Jennie said, a dreamy light in her eyes. "It sounds so exotic, so far away. What do you think it will be like?"

"I don't really know," Nathan replied. She looked so soft and wistful right then, he couldn't help experiencing a stab of guilt. None of this was her fault. Indeed, he should berate himself for being a bastard and a cad, after what he'd just done. "I know it's been settled a long time—longer than Boston, or Philadelphia, or New York."

"Really? I suppose I always thought of that part of the world as being open and undeveloped, with nothing much there except desert…and wild Indians, I suppose."

"I don't know how 'wild' they are in this day and age," he said, "but I expect we will see some Indians. But the Spaniards have been in New Mexico territory since the late sixteenth century."

"It will be fascinating, I'm sure." Jennie moved closer, shyly reached out to take his hand. He didn't dare resist, although he prayed she couldn't detect anything of Hannah's presence around him. The McAllister witch hadn't worn any scent that he had been able to perceive…unlike Jennie, whose hair was faintly perfumed with a trace of lilies. This close, the scent was almost cloying, and he tried not to cough. "Nathan…."

"Yes?" he asked, praying she wouldn't lift her

face to his for a kiss. In the past, he had found kissing her pleasant enough. Now, though, with Hannah McAllister's touch still lingering on his lips, he found the idea of being so intimate with his fiancée slightly distasteful. In time, he should get past that reticence. But not in this moment. Not when he had kissed Hannah only an hour earlier.

"Emma and I have been talking, and…."

Oh, dear God, what now? Nathan loved his sister dearly, but she did have a tendency to meddle in her brothers' lives more than Nathan believed she ought to. Too bad she didn't yet have a child of her own to keep her occupied, as Grace did, but then, Emma and Aaron hadn't even been married a year yet. Plenty of time to get a family started, and at this point they might as well wait until the Wilcox clan was safely established out west.

Pushing aside his irritation, he asked as mildly as he could, "Yes?"

"We were thinking—that is, she thought that perhaps it might be better if you and I were to get married here in New York before we set out on our travels. I know we had always meant to wait until we were away from New England, that we should start our new life together in a new place, but…." Jennie hesitated, her slender fingers tightening on his. Her brown eyes were wide, innocent…beseeching. "But there are so many grand churches in New York. I can't help but think we could have a proper wedding here, instead of some makeshift out in the territories. Why, I don't even know if we'll be able to find a preacher when the time comes."

Panic had begun to thrum through Nathan's body as soon as Jennie launched into this speech, but he forced himself to remain still and calm. The last thing he wanted was for her to discover how unappetizing this plan of hers sounded to him. "We are already very busy, Jennie," he said, his tone calm, soothing…and, he hoped, persuasive. "While I can understand why the idea of a church wedding here in New York would be appealing, I don't think any of us have the time to plan something like that. I truly believe it's better to wait—and I don't think you need to worry about finding someone to marry us once we're out west. Why, I've always heard that the first thing that gets built in any new settlement is the church, and of course you can't have a church without a preacher."

Her expression had turned quite somber as he made his reply, but she drew in a breath, then nodded. "I suppose you are right. Because I don't have all that much to do while we wait here, I sometimes forget that you and your brothers are so very busy, trying to get our travels planned for us. I can wait." She went up on her tiptoes, but at least she only placed her lips on his cheek, rather than attempting to kiss him on the mouth. No doubt she was trying to avoid being caught by any of his brothers or his sisters-in-law; the flat was not all that small, but with eight people and an infant occupying the space, it did rather lack for privacy.

"I know it's difficult," he said, and reached out so he could touch her cheek. Her skin was very soft. Indeed, Jennie Winfield was a pretty young woman in her own right. It was not her fault that he couldn't love her in the way that she deserved…not her fault that he couldn't help but contrast her placid sweetness with Hannah McAllister's passion and fire. "But I do believe we will be leaving soon enough, and once we're on the road, we'll be at our destination before you know it. Then we'll have a fine wedding, and an even better celebration afterward, because we will be able to toast our marriage and our new life at the same time."

"Thank you, Nathan." She touched his hand briefly, offered him another smile, and then retreated back into her room.

He passed a hand through his hair and swore at himself. What an utter bastard he was. At the moment, he thought he was definitely living up to the Wilcox reputation, however undeserved he might have once considered it.

The problem was—as much as he should have been doing his utter best to push Hannah McAllister out of his mind—all he could think about was how her mouth had felt on his, how she made him feel alive in a way he'd never thought possible. He didn't want to ponder what cruel fate had caused their paths to cross. If he had never met her, then he could have gone on to a pleasant, placid life with Jennie Winfield. He would never have known what he was missing.

And now—

The sound of footsteps made him startle. He looked up to see Jeremiah approaching, a sheaf of papers in one hand. His brother's brows drew together. Clearly, he must be wondering what on earth Nathan was doing, standing in the middle of the hallway like that. "Did you need to speak to me?"

"No," Nathan said quickly. "Jennie asked me to go on an errand for her, so I was wondering whether I should inquire and see if anyone else needed anything."

"I could use more ink, if you're going out." Jeremiah's dark eyes narrowed slightly as he regarded his brother. "Is something wrong?"

An echo of what Jennie had asked earlier. Nathan told himself that he needed to practice guarding his emotions, for clearly his encounter with Hannah McAllister had left its mark on him. He did not want to have to explain himself to Jeremiah, for the family patriarch and *primus* would most likely have little use for someone who pined over a woman he could never have.

With what he hoped was a casual lift of his shoulders, Nathan replied, "No, nothing is wrong."

"Hmm." Jeremiah hesitated for a moment, as though he intended to say something further. But then he seemed to give a mental shrug, and went on, "Be judicious in your purchases. Only what we absolutely need. I nearly have our plans finalized, and think we should be on the road no later than Monday next."

Four days. Four days, and they would be gone from this place. Hannah would be left behind, nothing more than a bittersweet memory, a hope for what might have been.

"Good," Nathan said. "Then I was right to tell Jennie there would be no time."

"Time for what?"

"A wedding."

Jeremiah let out an ironic chuckle. "Dear lord. She will have to wait, just as we had already planned. I trust you can also cool your heels for that much longer, little brother?"

Nathan wouldn't allow himself to chafe at the

"little brother" remark. After all, it was only the truth. By now he should be used to the good-natured way all his brothers didn't take him quite seriously. His magical gift was a useful one, but not at all flashy, and that didn't help matters much. Perhaps if he'd been able to fling fireballs at those who enjoyed teasing him, then he could have gotten a bit more respect.

"Yes, I think so," he said. "The important thing is to get the hell out of New York."

"I had no idea you disliked it so much."

"Oh, yes," Nathan replied immediately. "I most certainly do."

5

HANNAH HADN'T QUITE FORGOTTEN SO MUCH of herself that she neglected to run her errands on the way back to her clan's rented flat. Once she returned, she dutifully dispensed needles and thread, tooth powder and soap, and then retreated to her room.

She supposed she should be glad that she had this space to herself; most of the other rooms were occupied by two or even three or four people, but that was because they all formed their own nuclear families, husband and wife and children. Her brother Ian was bunking with their cousins Alastair and Timothy, for both of them were orphans, their parents lost in the feud with the McDougalls, and so had no one else to travel with them. She, however, was the only unattached female. Her Uncle Joseph had hesitated to bring her on this initial journey at all, only he did not want to separate her from her brother, not with both their parents gone. And expeditions of this sort could use her talents as a healer, since one never knew when a member of the party might meet with sickness or accident while on the road.

Besides, Cousin Mary was now quite far gone with child. Everyone hoped she would be able to hang on until they reached the Arizona Territories, but if not, then Hannah would be expected to oversee the delivery of the baby. She had already done so several times, although she did not look forward to the experience. Childbirth was loud and messy and painful, even when managed by a healer. Truly, she was somewhat surprised by the strength of her desire for Nathan Wilcox, when she knew exactly where such desire would inevitably lead.

Well, it didn't have to be inevitable. She knew the charm from the goddess Brigid, the one that would protect her from unwanted pregnancies. If the situation had arisen, she could have uttered the words and been as wanton and indiscreet as she liked, with no untoward consequences.

Unfortunately, she very much doubted she would be given the opportunity to be indiscreet with Nathan. Not after the way she had stormed at him and then stalked off. She wished she could blame her temper on her red hair, but she knew her hair had nothing to do with it at all.

And while she would like to say she had every reason to be angry with him, now that she had had an opportunity to cool down, she knew he had only been trying to be truthful. Surely she would be a hypocrite if she condemned him for being unfaithful to his fiancée, when she had done precisely the same thing. If only Boyd had been tall and dashing and handsome, like Nathan Wilcox! Then she would never have even looked at another man. As it was, she knew she must blame herself for her weakness. It was not fair to make this Boyd's fault, as he had been born who he was, and could do little to change that.

She was subdued at dinner that night, so quiet, that Uncle Joseph, ever the perceptive one, asked if she was feeling poorly. "For ye look a bit peaked, if ye don't mind the observation."

Of course she minded the observation, although she didn't dare tell him that. Joseph respected her talents and tried to be mindful of her lonely position in the world, but he was not the sort to brook any pertness, especially when his own position in the clan was so ambiguous. But with Hannah's cousin Caitriona looking wan and tragic next to him, and utterly unable to do much more than agree to whatever he suggested, Joseph was basically the head of the clan, no matter what the traditions might say.

"It was warm today," she said, and quickly popped a forkful of mashed potatoes into her mouth so she wouldn't have to say anything else.

Joseph had given her a piercing glance, one of those blue-grey stares that felt as though it was boring right through her, but he said nothing else, apparently deciding that the topic wasn't worth pursuing. Hannah had given out a little breath of relief, and then fled upstairs as soon as she was done with her part of clearing away the supper dishes.

Now she sat on the window seat and stared out at the skyline of New York, at all those windows flickering with gaslight or candlelight. The moon had just risen, was a bright yellow-white orb shining down on the city. Their rented flat was nowhere near Central Park, and yet she imagined the light of the moon shimmering off the pond there. Did people walk in the moonlight in the park? Did lovers use its uncertain illumination to hide themselves away and steal what kisses they could?

She and Nathan hadn't needed the encouragement of moonlight to share stolen kisses. No, they'd dared to do such a thing in the full blaze of a springtime sun. What foolhardiness that had been. She could only thank the Goddess that no one had been around to witness those embraces.

By Blessed Brigid, she needed to find a way to stop thinking about the man. These hours of separation didn't seem to have helped at all. If anything, her need to see him, to feel his arms again, had only increased. *Forbidden fruit*, the scowling Presbyterians back home would have said. She was only feeling the fires of sin.

But Hannah and her clan didn't believe in such things. It was no sin to love a person, to share physical pleasures. However, it was a sin to lie, to be dishonest and double-dealing. Wherever her parents had gone, into the next world beyond the veil, she hoped they could not see her now. Stealing away to see someone who should have been strictly forbidden. A man who, if not married, was still engaged, and therefore not someone she should have ever kissed.

She closed her eyes, shutting out that bright, alluring moon, and leaned her head against the window frame. A deep breath, and then another. This would pass. Sometime soon, she would regain her sanity. Perhaps there might come a day when she would laugh at herself, at her youthful foolishness.

Now, though, it only hurt.

A tingle at the back of her neck. Hannah opened her eyes and sat up straight, then glanced around her empty room with some bewilderment. That tingle had told her another witch or warlock was near, and yet she should not have experienced such a thing merely because of proximity to her family, whom she knew far too well. Which meant....

She flattened her hands against the small, square glass panes and peered out into the darkness. The street was illuminated by gas lamps placed at regular intervals, and yet she still couldn't see all that much. From somewhere around the corner she thought she heard the steady *clop-clop* of a horse's hooves, but here in Stuyvesant Street, all was still.

And yet —

There. Her eyes strained, and she realized that one of the shadows she'd spied beside the tree planted next door wasn't a shadow at all, but a tall man, all in black.

A long black coat.

Nathan.

Her heart leapt, even as she pulled in a worried breath and glanced back toward the hallway, sure that someone else would have noted the presence of the strange warlock, and gone down to see what he wanted. However, all seemed quiet, save for a low murmur of voices from the back room where Uncle Joseph had set up a small office. No doubt he was speaking with some of the men, making plans for the next day.

Knowing she hadn't a moment to lose, Hannah got up from the window seat, hurried into the hall, and then tiptoed down the stairs, glad that she had changed out of her fine bustle gown, which would have rustled all the way down those stairs, and into a plain dark skirt and white blouse. It was not nearly as becoming as the gown, of course, but it would be dark out on the street anyway.

She turned the knob and let herself out, then closed the front door behind her. Down the shallow, wide steps, and over toward the tree. A pair of strong arms reached out to catch her, and then she was pulled close, held so tightly that she knew she would have a difficult time getting away.

Not that she wanted to. This was all she wanted—the feel of Nathan Wilcox embracing her, something about the scent of wool and smoke that already seemed to be uniquely him, as though a thousand strangers could embrace her, and she would still be able to tell which man was him.

His voice murmured at her ear, "Oh, Hannah…I tried to stay away. But I couldn't. If you tell me to go, I will. But…I did not want to part on such terms, with words spoken in anger."

She reached up and tangled her hands in his thick hair, pulled him down to her so they might kiss. This was the answer she wanted to give—their lips locked together, bodies pressed so closely that surely any onlookers would have been utterly scandalized. But Hannah knew they were alone, that no one else walked this dimly lit street. After a long moment, she pulled away, then said, "I do not want to part at all."

A long pause. His hands grasped hers, warm. Now she could truly feel him, whereas this afternoon those dratted gloves had kept them from touching flesh to flesh. She could just see the gleam of his eyes in the darkness, the sorrow in them. "I fear we must. My brother has just informed me that we will be leaving next Monday."

It was as though he had punched her in the stomach. Suddenly, her stays were far too tight, cutting off what little air she could gasp in. She put a hand against the tree trunk to steady herself, felt the roughness of its bark beneath her fingers. That helped a little, helped to remind her of who she was, where she stood. They could not continue this conversation here, not so close to the house.

"Walk with me," she commanded, and began to head away from their rented flat, toward the far more bustling sidewalks of Third Avenue.

Nathan did not argue, but went with her, as if guessing the reason why she would want to put some distance behind them. Only once they had turned the corner and allowed themselves to fall in with the crowds walking there did he speak. "I know this is not welcome news…."

"It was expected," she said. What else could she tell him? He'd already informed her of his family's plans, and she had done the same. They were only two strangers who had somehow managed to cross paths in this enormous city.

No, not strangers. He would never be a stranger to her, this man who had awakened the fire in her heart.

"Still…."

At the sound of his voice, so rich and somehow soothing, as though it was honey and sunlight combined, she felt herself melt a little more inside. It was not fair. She knew it to be an absolute truth that she should be with Nathan Wilcox, not her cousin Boyd. And yet, what on earth could they do about it?

Even as that despairing question crossed her mind, another thought began to form, one so wild, so dangerous, she was not sure she dared to utter it. And yet, if Nathan agreed, what could either of their families do about the situation?

She slid her arm through the crook of his elbow and leaned in close. "Do you hate the very idea of leaving me?"

"You know I do, even though some would say

it is madness to feel this way about someone I barely know. And yet...you must feel the same, or you would not be here with me."

"I do feel the same. And if hearts are to be trusted, then we must trust ours now." She stopped next to another tree, this one a wide-spreading elm. No one appeared to be around them now, despite the crowds that had lingered at the intersection of Third Avenue and Stuyvesant Street. She swallowed a gulp of cool night air, knowing that what she was about to say to him very well could be considered utterly insane...and also knowing that if she did not make the suggestion now, she would regret it for the rest of her life. "If we confront our families with something we've already done, then there isn't anything they can do about it, is there?"

He stared at her, puzzlement evident on every feature, even in the dim flicker of the gas lamps. "Whatever are you talking about, Hannah?"

"Let us slip away tomorrow and get married. We can do it at City Hall. I do not need permission—I am of age, and both my parents are dead. Once we are married, what can our families do? They must accept the situation."

Nathan was silent so long, she feared he might not reply at all. Perhaps she had gone too far, and he thought her completely mad. And perhaps he would be right in that. It was a sweet madness, though, one that gave her hope for a future she didn't dread.

When he replied, however, his tone was gentle enough. "And what do you propose to do afterward?"

"Why, I would travel west with you and your family," she said. "Isn't that how it's usually done?"

"And your fiancé?"

"What of him?" she returned, wishing she felt quite as brave as she sounded. For while she certainly did not wish to marry Boyd, neither did she want to hurt him. Yes, there were undoubtedly other young women in the clan who would be happy enough to be his wife, who would overlook his lack of physical charms to be with someone that closely connected to the *prima,* but he would have to live his whole life knowing that his true betrothed had thrown him over for someone else. Could she do that to him, even if she didn't love him?

Yes, she thought, staring up at Nathan, at his troubled dark eyes, the mouth that seemed far more kissable than any other mouth she'd ever seen. She could do that...if it was for Nathan. Perhaps someday Boyd would forgive her. And perhaps he would even thank her, for with their engagement broken, he would be free to find someone who might care for him as himself. She couldn't quite imagine anyone being as madly in love with her cousin Boyd as she believed herself to be with Nathan Wilcox, but she supposed it was possible.

"You do not seem as though you fear you might break his heart, that is for certain," Nathan observed dryly, and she looked away, not quite certain that he wasn't teasing her.

"He doesn't love me," she said. She had spoken simply, without pathos. It was only the truth. From time to time she had wondered whether perhaps he might have loved her, if she'd given him the chance. Now she knew such a thing wasn't possible. Whatever magic it was that drew one person to another, it simply did not exist between them. "Nor I him. It was a match that was expedient for the clan, and nothing more."

"Well, I am glad to know that your conscience would be clear. I, however…."

He did not finish the sentence, and Hannah's heart sank. Such hesitation could only mean he did not agree with her. Yes, he might have said he did not love his fiancée, but clearly he cared enough that he would not disgrace her in such a way.

"You will marry someone you do not love?" Hannah asked, making no effort to keep the hurt —and, yes, the scorn—from her tone.

His brows drew together, and the light was not dim enough to hide the way his jaw clenched.

"I did not say that. It is only…Jennie is blameless in this. What's more, I know she cares for me, even if I cannot return that affection in the way she wishes. Still, my situation is not quite the same as yours, for at least in your case, you know that your cousin is as disinterested as you are."

What could she say to such a comment? Boyd's pride might be hurt, but nothing more. But this Jennie—Hannah wanted to hate her, and yet could not. How could she blame Jennie for caring about Nathan, when he was so easy to love? If her own fiancé had been even half as admirable, Hannah would have fallen in love with him, too. As it was….

"I know I am asking a great deal," she said. Her hand stole into Nathan's; to her relief, he took it, clasped it tightly. "And I know there are many who would think I am a terrible woman for even considering such a thing. But if we part here, my heart will break. Will Jennie's, if you beg off from your engagement?"

"I cannot say for sure." With his free hand, he reached out and touched her cheek, so gently that Hannah might have imagined the caress, if she had not witnessed it for herself. "Hers is a reserved sort of nature. She keeps much to herself. Certainly she is not given to wild flights of joy, or of despair. Whether someone with such a nature can suffer a broken heart…I simply don't know.

But…." He hesitated, and Hannah could feel the way his fingers tightened on hers. "I do know that I can't imagine a future without you in it, Hannah McAllister. Does that sound odd, when we have known each other for such a little time?"

She didn't think it odd at all. Many witches and warlocks experienced, if not love at first sight, at least a strong attraction early on. It was why most of them married quite young. "It is not the length of the acquaintance but the strength of it, I think."

Clearly, Nathan was in agreement, because he pulled her toward him then, was kissing her again, his mouth so strong, so demanding, that all Hannah could do was surrender to his caresses, let him hold her close in every abandonment of propriety there might be, to embrace on a street corner with all of New York to see what they were doing. Very well, perhaps not all of New York, but still, it was a very public place.

And she didn't care. In fact, some part of her was glad that he kissed her here and now, because certainly any of these proper Americans would think she was compromised, and therefore Nathan could do nothing except marry her to restore her honor.

When he let her go, she could hear his harsh breathing, could see the wild glitter of his eyes in the lamplight.

"Yes, Hannah," he said. "Let us get married. Tomorrow, before anything in either of our situations can change. I will arrange everything. Can you meet me once again in Central Park?"

She nodded. "I'm sure I can come up with some errand that will safely take me out of the house."

"And bring your things with you?"

"'My things'?" she repeated, not quite understanding what he had meant.

"Perhaps not everything you brought with you from Scotland, but a small valise, so you will have the necessities for a night away. After all," he added, with a wicked smile that made her knees go weak, "what is a wedding without a wedding night?"

6

THIS WAS UTTER MADNESS. NATHAN KNEW that, knew he was committing an unpardonable sin against his betrothed, against his clan...and yet, he didn't care. After kissing Hannah once again, feeling her in his arms, her lithe body pressed up against him, he knew he could be with no one else. He would make his amends to Jennie somehow, but he would not be deterred from having Hannah McAllister as his wife.

Luckily, everyone had retired to their rooms for the evening by the time Nathan returned from his encounter with Hannah, and so no one had the opportunity to ask him where he had been and what he had been doing. No doubt Jeremiah knew the precise moment when his younger brother stepped across the threshold, but he did not emerge from the room he shared with his wife

Lisbeth. If he wondered at all, Jeremiah probably thought Nathan had simply stepped out for a drink at the bar around the corner. Each of the brothers had done so more than once, so it made a good excuse.

In the morning, the flat was a-bustle, for now that Jeremiah had settled on the date of their departure, there was much to be done. Packing was already commencing, of the items that wouldn't be immediately needed over the next few days. And Jeremiah asked Nathan to go to the rail yard, so he might inspect the accommodations on the westward-bound train, and determine whether the extra expense of a first-class compartment was worth it.

Of course Nathan agreed to this fact-finding mission, as it would get him safely away without having to offer any explanations for an extended absence. He would take care of that errand first, and then go to City Hall afterward to procure the marriage license. After that, he would meet Hannah, and return with her to have the ceremony performed. And then…

…and then she would be his wife.

A rush of heat went through him at that thought. Her kisses were sweet, and he could only imagine what it would be like to have all of her. Surely that same passion must carry over to her marriage bed.

Trying to be a dutiful brother, he visited the rail yard, where a slightly puzzled conductor allowed him to peek inside one of the empty trains. Nathan took notes, but it was clear enough to him that the family would be terribly cramped unless they bought passage in one of the first-class cars. Because they would be spending two days on the train, the extra expense would be worth it.

And we will be one more, he thought as he thanked the conductor and headed out toward the street, *so we will have need of all the space we can procure.*

No, that wasn't right. He couldn't imagine that Jennie would remain with them and still head west. Once she learned of his betrayal, she would demand to be sent home to her family in Connecticut. At least, that was what Nathan knew he would do if he were in similar circumstances. However, he had never seen Jennie lose her temper, so he had to admit he was at something of a loss as to how she might behave. He did have the idea that she would look at him with reproach in those big brown eyes of hers, and he could not blame her for that. In a way, he hoped she would lose her temper, get angry, call him every terrible name she could think of. He deserved nothing less. And when she was done, they could both move on with their lives.

He went to get the license, trying not to curse

at the line which greeted him at City Hall. The bored-looking clerk informed him that the judge stopped performing ceremonies promptly at four, but if he was not able to return by then, the clerk could offer the names of a few accommodating ministers…for a small fee.

Nathan couldn't help but grin. "No fear," he told the clerk. "My fiancée and I will be here in plenty of time. But thank you for the information."

The clerk shrugged. "Then best of luck to you, sir."

Smiling, Nathan slipped the license into his breast pocket and went back outside. The day was not quite as sunny as the one before, but in a way that was good, because the air was slightly cooler, the breeze crisp and comfortable. He pulled out his pocket watch and gave it a quick glance. Nearly two-thirty. He was to meet Hannah at three, so he had a little time.

Across the street was a jewelry store. Perfect. After waiting impatiently for a break in the traffic, he hurried over to the shop, which had all sorts of gleaming enticements placed in the front window. While he did not have a great deal of money to spare, he knew he should buy a ring for Hannah. Nothing too ostentatious, but something she would be proud to wear.

There. In the second display case was a gold

band with a delicate engraved pattern set with small grass-green emeralds and tiny diamonds. Those emeralds were just the color of her eyes, and since so far he'd only seen her wear shades of green or blue, he thought the ring should do very well with her wardrobe.

When he asked the salesclerk the price, it was high, but not so terribly high that he couldn't afford to part with the cash. He willingly pulled the silver dollars from his pocket and handed them over, then watched as the clerk put the ring in a satin-lined box and tied it up with a ribbon.

This mission thus accomplished, Nathan went on his way, hailing a cab so he might arrive a little early at his destination. The park was nearly as crowded as it had been the day before, and all the benches near the carousel were already occupied. Very well. Being able to sit down did not matter that much, since he and Hannah would be on their way as soon as she arrived.

And there she was, coppery curls gleaming, the feathers on her straw hat dancing gaily in the breeze. Today she wore again the blue dress she'd had on when he first saw her, her slender waist reduced almost to nothingness by the yards and yards of ruffled cotton. Nathan couldn't help but note the way some of the men standing by the carousel glanced over in her direction, gazes sharpening with interest.

However, she didn't appear to notice any of them, but sailed through the crowd until she was at his side. Her green eyes were filled with excitement as she reached out to take his hand.

"Have you been waiting long?"

"Not at all," he replied. "Did you have any trouble getting away?"

"No, thank goodness. One of the babies had the croup, and I had to manage that before I could leave. Luckily, though, everyone was so relieved that Johnny had quieted down, no one said anything when I told them I wanted to go back to Macy's to match some ribbon to a gown I was making over."

"That is a relief." And, he thought, a clever choice of errand, since he could not think of anything more calculated to keep Hannah's brother from her side.

"Oh, I know. It also gave me the perfect excuse to bring my valise with me, for how else could I carry my gown?" From beneath the billowy masses of her ruffled overskirt, she produced a small, worn case of dark brown leather. "Of course, it might have a *few* more things in it than just that gown."

"You are a marvel," he said, and bent and kissed her forehead. "We should go now, though, because the judge will only marry us up until four o'clock. We had best take a cab."

"Such extravagance," she teased, although Nathan thought he also detected a bit of anticipation in her voice. From what he'd been able to tell, the McAllisters were not terribly well off. They would think of cab rides as extravagances—and would also, no doubt, think the same thing of the ring he had in his pocket. Why bother with emeralds and diamonds when a plain gold band would do just as well?

It was not much work to hail a cab. Within fifteen minutes, they were standing on the steps of City Hall, Hannah looking up at the neoclassical columns with some awe. Very likely there hadn't been anything remotely like the building back in her village in Scotland, although she should have begun to get used to such sights by now.

When she spoke, though, he realized it wasn't the magnificence of the building that had cowed her, but the enormity of what they were about to do.

"You're sure?" she whispered, hands tight on the handle of her valise.

"I've never been more certain about anything else," he said. "But if you're having second thoughts—"

"No," she said quickly. "I—I want to. I do. It's just…up until this moment, it didn't feel quite real."

"I understand." He leaned down so he could

kiss her cheek, and she flushed slightly. "You are real, though. You are more real than anyone I've ever met."

She smiled then, the sort of smile that made her green eyes sparkle in a manner to put the emeralds in the ring he'd bought her to shame. "You are, too, Nathan. You are…everything."

"Then let us add 'husband' to that everything, shall we?"

A nod, and she freed one hand from her valise so she might put it in his as they walked up the steps, then went inside the building. There was now something of a line to see the judge, but not, Nathan hoped, long enough that it would keep them from ending this afternoon in the way that they had planned. He and Hannah stood out among those petitioners, too; many of them were plainly, even shabbily dressed, immigrants too poor to afford a church service, or those from the city's lower classes, wishing to make their relationships formal, even if they could do nothing more than say a few words in front of a judge.

Some of the women looked at Hannah's fancy bustle dress and nodded to themselves. Did they think he had disgraced her, and was now forcing her into a quick marriage? Nothing could be further from the truth, of course. Also, while Hannah's gown might look quite modish to these women, Nathan knew from the dresses the women in his family wore that it was not really so very fancy—the collar was hand-tatted lace, and the fabric a plain cotton with a shadow stripe woven into the fabric, certainly not silk brocade.

In this company, the woman who was about to become his wife seemed far more subdued, her expression anxious, her gaze not meeting his—or anyone else's. Once again her hands were wrapped tightly around the handle of her valise, the knuckles almost white. As much as he wanted to reassure her, he also felt the need to remain silent. Certainly they could not talk of their families, or their future plans. Not when surrounded by nonmagical folk such as these. Anyway, there would be plenty of time in the future to speak of such things.

The line moved far more slowly than he would have liked, but in the end, they finally reached the chambers of the man who would make them husband and wife. He was a tired-looking individual, with a drooping hound-dog face and prodigious bags under his eyes. However, the smile he offered Hannah appeared genuine enough as he asked for the license.

Nathan produced it from his breast pocket. The judge inspected it briefly, then nodded toward an equally tired-looking woman who sat on a hard chair off to one side. "Mrs. Lawkins here will act as your witness, if you've brought no family with you."

"Thank you," Nathan said, but offered no explanation beyond that. The last thing he wanted to do was provide any details as to why he and his fiancée were here completely unaccompanied.

It seemed the judge had seen this sort of a thing many times before, because he only nodded. "Then we'll go ahead and get started. *Dearly beloved….*"

Nathan knew the words of the ceremony well enough; he had sat through the weddings of his sister and his three older brothers. This time, though, he wanted to focus on every word, every phrase, for they rang with far more significance now than they ever had before. Was it possible that the beautiful woman standing next to him was about to become his wife, someone he hadn't known even existed three days ago?

Apparently it was possible, for there was Hannah, calmly repeating the familiar words of the ceremony, although in a voice that trembled here and there, as if she, too, was acknowledging the enormity of what they were doing.

Then the judge said, "The ring, please."

Nathan reached in his other pocket and produced the box, then pulled out the jewel-studded band he had bought only an hour earlier. "With this ring, I thee wed." He slipped it onto

Hannah's finger; it fit so perfectly, she might as well have been with him when he selected it.

Her eyes widened. "Nathan, it's beautiful."

"I'm glad you like it."

The judge cleared his throat. "If we might continue…?"

Hannah blushed. "Of course."

There wasn't that much left to say. Only a few more exchanges, and at last the judge intoned, "I now pronounce you man and wife. You may kiss the bride."

Nathan needed no encouragement. He bent and touched his lips to Hannah's, wondering again at the sweet fire such kisses awoke, even one as chaste as this, with these two impersonal onlookers. She gazed up at him, eyes shining, as the judge said, "Congratulations, Mr. and Mrs. Wilcox."

For a moment, Nathan could only stare down at Hannah. Mrs. Wilcox. His wife. This amazing creature, this miracle who had somehow appeared in his life.

Then he kissed her again, fervently enough that the judge once more cleared his throat and said, "It is almost four, and there is still one couple I need to see. If perhaps you could continue that outside—"

"Of course." Nathan looped his arm in Hannah's and led her out of the judge's chambers.

As he'd said, there was still one couple waiting, both of whom appeared almost as tired as the judge himself. They looked on incuriously as the newlyweds passed them by, but Nathan could spare no further thoughts for them, or anyone except the woman whose arm he held. His wife.

They emerged into a day that had turned mostly grey. Now the breeze felt almost cold, although he noticed Hannah didn't seem to mind. She lifted her head into the wind, her long curls blowing behind her like copper streamers, then turned to look up at him.

"So what do we do now? Go home and break the news?"

That was the sensible thing to do. It wasn't as if he and Hannah would be able to hide what they had done. But Nathan didn't want to take the glow off the afternoon quite so soon. They should be allowed to enjoy themselves for a little longer, before reality came crashing in on them.

He fingered the coins in his pocket. There should be enough, he judged, to get the two of them a room at one of the city's finest hotels. Surely they could be allowed one night together; that was what he had envisioned when he asked Hannah to bring her valise. But no, doing so would only cause more problems than it would create. If he didn't return home—if Hannah seemed to have disappeared into thin air—then both witch clans would tear the city apart looking for them.

Hannah appeared to sense his hesitation, for she reached out and touched his arm. "What is the matter, Nathan?"

"I thought of giving us a proper wedding night," he said, "but I know that if we were to be gone overnight, we would cause even more consternation among our families. We can steal a few hours at most, nothing more."

"Oh." She appeared to consider for a moment. "But if we were to go stay at a hotel, perhaps we wouldn't have to be there all night. I know it sounds extravagant, but—"

"No, that is the perfect solution." He would take her to the Astoria. It was somewhat declined from its heyday, but still grand enough. And perhaps there it wouldn't be noticed that the newlyweds who had let a room did not stay around for breakfast. Even if someone did notice, what would it matter? They would be gone from this city soon enough, never to return. He offered her a smile. "I know exactly where we should go."

7

HANNAH WAS QUITE SURE SHE HAD NEVER seen such luxury. Their room had a fine patterned carpet from wall to wall, and gleaming draperies of silk damask, and furniture of rich mahogany. It was like a place where a princess might stay, rather than plain Hannah McAllister from Halkirk, Scotland.

No longer Hannah McAllister, though. Now she was Hannah Wilcox, with surely the finest husband the world had ever seen. He stood there now, thanking the bellhop who had brought up a tray of delectable dishes from the hotel's restaurant, along with a bottle of champagne. After discreetly handing the man a coin, Nathan closed the door behind him, leaving them alone at last. He went to the tray and retrieved the flutes of cut crystal, and handed one to her.

She took it awkwardly by the stem; she'd never held a glass like this before. The mere sight of the champagne entranced her, the way the fine bubbles fizzed up from the bottom of the glass, endlessly moving through the pale straw-colored liquid.

"To our future," Nathan said, raising his glass, "and the combined futures of the Wilcox and McAllister clans."

Lifting her glass in return, Hannah realized what Nathan had just said was more than a toast. For better or worse, the two witch clans would always be entwined from here on out, because she and Nathan were now joined. She wondered if the Wilcoxes would now decide to settle in Flagstaff, so they wouldn't be too far away from the McAllisters in Jerome.

But she could worry about all that later. For now, it was enough that she was here with Nathan. She put the champagne flute to her lips, took a small swallow. The alcohol fizzed in her mouth, so much lighter and more delicate than cider. Indeed, drinking it made her feel quite wicked, like she was now a woman of the world.

"To the future," Hannah echoed. Oh, she'd gotten that wrong, hadn't she? She was supposed to make the toast first, then drink.

Nathan didn't seem to notice. He sipped again

at his champagne, then set the flute down on the table next to him so he might inspect the tray of delicacies that had been placed there. "Which would you like first, Hannah? One of these oyster patties, or perhaps one of these crepes with shellfish?"

Since she had no idea what either of those foods might taste like, she lifted her shoulders. "Whichever you would like me to try first."

"A crepe, I think." He used a wide silver spatula to transfer the thin pancake-like item to a smaller plate, then handed it to her, along with a fork.

She took it from him and waited as he dished up some for himself. After he gave her an encouraging smile, she allowed herself a small, cautious bite. The filling was so creamy and rich, and the pancake—the crepe—was light as air in contrast, providing just enough structure to prevent the shellfish mixture from spreading out all over her plate.

"Oh, that's delicious!" she exclaimed.

"I thought you might like it. And now try it with some champagne."

Obediently, she took another bite, then followed it with a mouthful of the fizzy drink. Nathan was right—they did make a marvelous combination. Clearly, he knew far more about fancy food and drink than she did.

And no doubt a good deal many other things as well.

A little shiver went over her. She couldn't quite rid herself of the feeling that they were doing something illicit, although of course it was entirely proper for a man and wife to be alone in a hotel room together. Something about the champagne made her feel decidedly improper, though. She swallowed some more, ate a few more bites of crepe, and realized that somehow she'd managed to empty her flute.

"More?" Nathan asked, picking up the bottle.

"Oh, yes, please. It's just lovely."

He smiled and refilled her glass, then did the same with his own flute. The room began to feel a bit fuzzy as a delightful lightheadedness started to steal over her. Was this how it felt to get drunk? She had always thought of drunkenness as something heavy-handed and rather vulgar, but she didn't feel vulgar. She felt…like she was floating on a cloud.

Then she realized Nathan had set down his champagne and had come over to her, had pushed the heavy fall of curls away from the back of her neck so he could lay his lips against the sensitive skin there. A delicious shiver stole over her, followed by a spreading warmth that seemed to touch all her limbs. And more than that, a sort of pulsing heat at the center of her body.

He murmured at her ear, "You trust me, don't you?"

She didn't even have to stop to consider. "Of course I do." How could she not trust him? She loved him with every cell in her body…a body that was telling her she wanted him to continue what he was doing. Anyway, she was not a complete innocent. Although she had never known a man's touch before this, she had grown up in the country, had seen animals together. She knew there would be some kind of a joining between them, even if she couldn't quite visualize how it was all supposed to work.

But that was all right. Nathan must know. He would show her.

His lips traveled down her neck, kissing her gently. As she pulled in a breath, his fingers began working the buttons down the front of her bodice, releasing her from its high-necked confines. She made no protest as he pulled the bodice away from her, tossed it onto one of the chairs. How could she protest when his mouth touched her there, moving lower, shifting her stays and chemise so her breast was now exposed? His tongue flicked over her, and she gasped aloud, startled by how amazingly, shockingly *good* that felt.

"Come to bed, my love," he said, and took her by the hands and raised her from the chair where she sat, then led her over to the bed, a massive mahogany four-poster piled high with pillows and the most luxurious feather mattress she had ever seen.

Now he was unhooking her bustled over-drape and the skirt beneath it, letting them fall to the carpeted floor. His fingers worked at the clasps on her corset, until it, too, was freed from her body. Never in her life had she been unclothed like this in front of a man, standing here only in her chemise and her pantalets and stockings. She kicked off her shoes, and let him pull the ribbon of her chemise loose so he might unbutton that as well. As his hands closed over her bare breasts, she gasped—but then she widened her eyes at him and said, "You are not being fair, Nathan."

"'Fair'?" he echoed, his voice rough with desire.

"Why, you have me nearly naked, and yet you stand there still in your coat and your vest and shirt. How is that fair?"

A quick grin blazed across his features. "You are right, of course. Then I shall have to remedy the situation."

Fingers moving in a flash, he removed the stickpin in his tie, then undid the length of silk and tossed it to one side. His coat followed, then his waistcoat, and at last his shirt. Hannah wanted to gasp again when she saw his unclothed torso, strong with muscle, his skin browned from the sun—or perhaps he was just naturally swarthy, to match his coal-black hair and eyes. His chest was smooth, though, not nearly as hairy as some of the men she'd seen working in the fields, their shirts removed so they might not overheat in the sun. They could not compare to his perfection, though. He looked like statues she'd seen in books of ancient Greek gods.

But he gave her no more time to drink him in, because then he was pushing her down against the bed, his bare chest pressed up against her breasts, his mouth claiming hers as they embraced. With one hand he pushed her chemise out of the way, then reached up to undo the drawstring of her pantalets. And oh, dear Goddess, his fingers were slipping into her, touching her in a place she'd done her best to ignore, making her feel like…she didn't even know, only that the blood in her veins seemed to have turned to honey, warm and golden and sweet.

She cried out, fingers digging into his muscled arms, as a wave of pleasure swept over her, one so intense that she wasn't quite sure she might not faint from its pure intensity. As she opened her eyes, she saw Nathan staring down into her face, dark eyes like endless midnight oceans.

"Was that good, my love?" he whispered.

All she could do was nod, for in that moment

she wasn't sure she was capable of actual speech. He ran a hand down the side of her face, those strong fingers so gentle, so adoring, and she closed her eyes again. Not because she didn't want to see his handsome face, but because she needed to dwell within her body for a moment longer, to savor the warm glow of its response.

She felt him move, and heard a rustle of cloth as he undid the buttons on his trousers and let them slide to the floor. When she opened her eyes again, it was to him tugging at her chemise so he could draw it over her head. He was completely naked now, and at the sight of him, a faint whisper of fear went through her. She hadn't imagined that he would be quite so…large.

It would be all right. He'd already made her feel better than she'd ever imagined she would, so she couldn't imagine him hurting her. She didn't protest as he pulled down her pantalets and cast them aside, presumably to fall on top of their other discarded clothing. His hands were on her again, caressing, gently sliding over her breasts, reaching down to that tantalizing spot between her legs. She could feel how wet she was down there, something she'd never really expected.

"I love you," he whispered.

"I love you, Nathan," she replied, her own voice a throaty murmur. "Go on. I—I want you to."

This coaxing made him close his eyes for a moment. "I want you, Hannah. God, how I want you."

She reached up to run a hand through his thick black hair. "Then show me."

He pulled in a breath, then shifted his weight slightly. She could feel him pressing against her, feel how hard and heavy he was. But because he'd pleasured her earlier, he slipped in more easily than she'd expected. Yes, there was a sudden, sharp twinge, and she had to bite her lip to keep from crying out, because she somehow knew that if she gave any sign he was hurting her, he might stop. She didn't want him to stop. Already it was beginning to feel better as he started to move in and out, slowly and gently. She wrapped her arms around him, holding him close as they rocked together, finding their rhythm, as she let him take her for his own, every stroke, every low moan proclaiming that now they had joined as one.

When he cried aloud and the climax took him, Hannah knew she should be saying the charm from Saint Brigid, the one that would keep her from conceiving. After all, wouldn't it be better to wait until after they were safely established in the Arizona Territories, or wherever else the Wilcoxes decided to settle?

But she didn't say the words, or even repeat them in her mind. If the Goddess saw fit to bless her with a child from this ecstatic union, how could Hannah say no? She would thank the Goddess, and be glad of this evidence of the love she and Nathan shared.

So when it was over, Hannah only held her husband close, and fell asleep in his arms.

8

A SLAM OF THE DOOR TO THEIR SUITE WOKE
Nathan from his stupor. He put a hand to his
head, then looked over to his right. There was
Hannah, the sheets barely covering her full
breasts, her hair a riot of copper against the pris-
tine white pillowcase.

Damn. How could he have allowed himself to
fall asleep? Yes, this room was theirs until late the
next morning, but he hadn't planned to stay
nearly so long. They had made love, then gotten
up and drunk the rest of the champagne and
finished off the tray of food…and then had
returned to bed, where they loved one another yet
again, this time more slowly, so they might
explore all the pleasures of their bodies.

And they had slept. One lamp in the parlor

had been lit, but Nathan could tell it was full dark outside the windows. Damn again.

He didn't have any time for recriminations beyond that, because in the next second a shadow passed in front of the parlor lamp, and Jeremiah stood in the open doorway to the bedroom, a ferocious scowl creasing his forehead.

"What the hell do you think you're doing?" he demanded. His furious gaze shifted to Hannah, who was somehow still miraculously asleep. "Who is that woman?"

"'That woman' is my wife," Nathan replied. The shock of seeing his brother had turned to anger as soon as he heard the condemnation in his voice. The expression on Jeremiah's face told him exactly what he thought of Hannah, and Nathan knew he had to make it very clear who she was, that she was not some woman of the street that he'd taken for a night's pleasure.

"Your wife?" Jeremiah thundered. This time, Hannah did stir and began to sit up—and then let out a startled gasp as she caught sight of the man who stood at the entrance to the bedroom. One hand quickly grasped the sheets before they could slip any further and reveal far more than she wished.

"Yes, my *wife,*" Nathan said. He had wanted these introductions to go far differently from this, but the damage was done. Now all he could do was attempt to salvage the situation. "Jeremiah, this is Hannah McAllister."

Despite her nearly naked state, she held herself with such dignity that Nathan thought he might fall in love with her all over again. Sheet clutched to her breast, she said proudly, "Hannah Wilcox, now. But I am from the McAllister clan."

Jeremiah's eyes narrowed. "I told you to observe her, Nathan, not marry her."

That comment made her sit up even straighter, but she didn't blink. "Are you trying to shock me with this revelation, sir? For Nathan already told me all about that."

"How very honorable of him," Jeremiah said. "Did he also tell you that he was already engaged to someone else?"

Nathan had never wanted to punch his brother in the jaw more than he did in that moment. However, he knew better than to provoke a physical confrontation—or a magical one. Jeremiah Wilcox was not someone you wanted to cross…even if he did happen to be your brother. "Yes, I did tell her," he said calmly. "I would never have married her without letting her know the truth first."

She sent him a warm smile. "And I thank you again for your honesty, Nathan." A lift of the chin, and she returned her attention to Jeremiah. "As for you, sir, since you are now my brother-in-law,

I will ignore the fact that you entered this suite without Nathan's permission. For the moment, however, I would very much appreciate it if you would give us some privacy so we might get dressed."

"Of course, ma'am," Jeremiah replied with a curl of the lip. "I will wait for you in the parlor."

Having delivered this ominous promise, he closed the door behind him. At once Nathan reached over and took Hannah's hand. "I am sorry. I had no idea that he would track me down here—"

"It's all right," she broke in. Judging by the dangerous sparkle in her green eyes, he was not sure whether it was, in fact, all right, but he knew better than to contradict her. "Or rather, it is not *your* fault that he came here. It does concern me that your brother was able to find you so easily, however."

"He has…many powers," Nathan said slowly, wishing he'd had more time to explain Jeremiah to her. And he cursed himself for a fool, both for allowing himself to fall asleep and also for not thinking that his brother would find a way to track him down when he'd gone missing for too long.

Hannah had been reaching down for her chemise and pantalets when he made that remark. She straightened and gave him a piercing look, even as she began to slide the pantalets up her slender legs. "What do you mean, 'many powers'? He has more than one gift?"

"Yes. That is, beyond all the common, small talents we of witch-kind share. But where you are a healer, and one of my other brothers can make himself travel from place to place in the blink of an eye, Jeremiah's ability is to change magic itself, to bend it to suit his will. Even I don't know everything of all the skills he has at his command."

Some of the pretty pink in her cheeks drained as Hannah appeared to take in this latest revelation. "He is a dangerous man, then."

"I am not sure if 'dangerous' is the right word. He has only used these powers to defend our clan, never to gain an advantage for himself."

"That you know of," she said darkly, and slipped the chemise over her head. Once thus clad, she came around to the other side of the bed and picked up her abandoned skirts and the heavy wired petticoat she wore beneath them.

"I don't think he would hide such things from us," Nathan replied, although even as he spoke, he wondered if he was being disingenuous. Jeremiah had already proven himself to be ruthless when the situation warranted it. If he had participated in activities that he thought might meet with disapproval from other members of the family, then there was a good chance he might simply omit any mention of them.

However, Nathan did not feel it was a good idea to speak of such things to Hannah, not when he didn't have any solid proof. The last thing he wanted was for her to be frightened of his older brother. Not that Jeremiah had helped his cause too much on that particular front, showing up here out of nowhere with a face like a storm cloud.

From the dubious expression Hannah currently wore, it seemed she was not altogether convinced, either. She did not bother to contradict him, but only remained focused on putting together her complicated ensemble, even as Nathan climbed into his trousers and drew on his shirt and waistcoat. He decided not to bother with his frock coat, and left it hanging over the arm of a chair. But he did pause to retrieve the marriage license from the inside breast pocket of the coat, just in case Jeremiah required concrete proof that his brother and the McAllister witch truly were married.

Hannah seemed to realize that re-creating her complex hairstyle would take far too long, and so she settled for running her fingers through her long curls, smoothing them as best she could, and then tying them back with a ribbon. With her hair like that, she suddenly appeared very young, far younger than the wanton woman who had made fierce love to him only a few hours earlier.

And Lord only knows what Jeremiah will think of that, Nathan reflected. *No doubt he'll accuse me of robbing the cradle, even though Hannah is a grown woman of twenty.*

There was no help for it, though. His brother waited for the two of them in the parlor of their suite, and the sooner they got this thrashed out, the better. In a way, as shocking and unwelcome as Jeremiah's appearance here had been, perhaps it could work to their advantage. They could talk over the situation amongst themselves, without the entire family listening in. And once Nathan had won over his brother, they would present a united front in explaining to Jennie what had happened, that it was none of her fault.

Yes, and then the angels will sing and rainbows will appear, he thought sourly. His brothers had often teased him for being too much of an optimist, but this was a sunny outlook even for him.

But still, it must be done.

He offered his arm to Hannah, who took it gratefully, her fingers looking very small and fragile as they clung to him. However, he knew she wasn't fragile. Not really. She had weathered losses and feuds and upsets of her own; she could weather this as well, especially with him at her side.

Jeremiah was standing by the unlit hearth, a slight frown of distaste pulling at his mouth as he looked at the detritus of their celebration from earlier—the tray with its denuded serving platters, the small plates with the scraps of food still sticking to them, the empty champagne bottle and the flutes now smudged with fingerprints. The frown did not lessen when he turned to look at the newlyweds, even though at least they were now properly attired.

"Do you wish to explain yourself, Nathan?" he said, again with that curl of the lip Nathan disliked so much. It always gave the impression that Jeremiah thought himself superior to everyone around him. True, his powers far outstripped those of any witch or warlock Nathan had ever met, but even so, it rankled.

"What is there to explain?" he countered. "I met Hannah, and we knew soon enough that we cared for one another. It is often like that among witch-kind, that we can quickly recognize the person most suitable for us. Or rather," he added, with a half-sneer of his own, as he let go of his bride and crossed his arms, "we can recognize that person if we are given the opportunity to do so, as long as our clans don't attempt to do our choosing for us, and instead ram the person they've selected down our throats."

Jeremiah showed no reaction to this barb, except to flick a speck of lint from the sleeve of his jacket. When his face went bland and expressionless like that, Nathan had learned it was better to stop, for it meant his brother was dangerously close to an explosion. The words could not be taken back now, however. "I wasn't aware any force was involved in your engagement to Jennie Winfield, brother. She was suggested to you, and you accepted readily enough."

"Because I didn't know the difference," Nathan protested. "Until I met Hannah, I—"

"You didn't understand true love?" Jeremiah drawled. "What a prodigy this new wife of yours must be, to make you suddenly comprehend an emotion that men have been puzzling over for centuries."

Beside him, Hannah planted her hands on her hips, green eyes blazing. "Spoken like a man who has never experienced it for himself. Your own lack should not influence what happens between your brother and me."

Damn. Although Nathan could not help but admire her spirit, he wished that Hannah had held her tongue. She had no true idea of who she was tangling with…and neither could she have any idea of how disappointed Jeremiah had been in his own marriage.

For a moment, Jeremiah did not reply. Then a smile touched his lips—a smile that, to anyone who knew him intimately, would immediately be recognized as an expression that did not bode well for its recipient. "You do speak your mind, don't you, Miss McAllister?"

"Mrs. Wilcox!" she flung back at him.

"Ah." Jeremiah's cool black gaze flicked toward his brother. "You won't be offended, Nathan, if I ask for some proof of this marriage?"

"Not at all. I thought you might." Nathan extended the folded-up marriage license in one hand, and Jeremiah took it, unfolded the piece of paper, and briefly scanned its contents.

"This does all seem to be in order," he said.

"Of course it is," Nathan retorted. "Do you think I would do anything to compromise the woman I love?"

"Most likely not." These harmless words were delivered in a tone that positively dripped with scorn, however. Nathan began to bristle, but did not have a chance to reply before Jeremiah went on, "And do you have any idea what you are going to say to Jennie? She is blameless, after all."

"I will explain as best I can," Nathan replied. He could not allow himself to relax, but he was glad to see that Jeremiah didn't look quite as angry as he had a few moments earlier. Perhaps when presented with the marriage license, he had understood he could not change what had happened. And the mention of Jennie seemed to indicate that the clan's *primus* was now ready to push past the immediate blow of Nathan's unexpected marriage in order to deal with the consequences.

"Oh, no doubt you will." Jeremiah paused to pull a watch from his waistcoat pocket. "It is not quite eight o'clock. Not late, but certainly late enough that your wife's clan members must be worried to death about her. This city is not safe for a woman alone…even a witch."

"I can do just fine on my own—" Hannah began to protest, but Jeremiah shook his head.

"You may believe that, but I have a feeling your family does not share that sentiment. I will see that you make it home safely."

"You will do no such thing," Nathan said. "She is my wife, and so it is my place to escort her to her family. Only," he added, as Hannah's eyes began to blaze with anger once again, "until I can get this matter sorted out with Jennie. I have already dealt her a blow, and to bring you home with me now would only increase the insult. Let me speak to her first, and then tomorrow we will be together."

"An excellent plan," Jeremiah said, a gleam in his eyes that Nathan didn't much like. He had the feeling that his brother was plotting something new, but he couldn't think what it might be. All he could do was remain wary and ready to counter any new offensives that might come his way. Breaking the news to both families would be difficult, but it must be done so that he and Hannah could begin their new life together. His brother went on, "Then Nathan, take Hannah home and explain the situation. When you are done, come back and speak with Jennie. After that we will have a better idea of what we must do next."

This plan sounded so eminently sensible that Nathan thought there must be something wrong with it. However, since he knew he would get nothing from Jeremiah unless it was freely volunteered, he decided it was best to go ahead and get this over with. A few hours of unpleasantness, and then the evening would be over, and he would be able to look forward to a new day. "We will go now." He glanced over at Hannah, whose expression was still somewhat mutinous. "Get your things, my love."

At least she didn't argue, but said meekly enough, "Of course, Nathan." She went back into the bedroom to fetch her valise and her hat. After she left, the tension in the room seemed somehow increased, rather than lessened.

"The hotel room—" Nathan began.

"I will take care of it," Jeremiah said smoothly.

"It will be late enough by the time you are done with the McAllisters. You shouldn't keep Jennie waiting until all hours."

Any protest against this plan would only make it sound as though he cared nothing for Jennie's sensibilities. Since he had already wounded her gravely—even if she didn't know that yet—Nathan kept silent, and only offered a curt nod.

A moment later, Hannah re-emerged, hat perched at a precarious angle on her head, valise in one hand. She looked precisely like a woman who had spent the last few hours engaged in illicit activities, but there was little they could do about it, except waste more valuable time while waiting for her to pin up her hair.

It seemed that Hannah realized this as well, because her expression was downright challenging, as if she expected to have to defend herself. That was why Nathan only went to her and took her valise, then said, "Come along, darling. It is time for me to meet your family."

Something about her posture seemed to falter somewhat, but then her chin came up again as she replied, "Yes, they do need to hear the news." Her gaze shifted to Jeremiah. "It was very nice to make your acquaintance, Mr. Wilcox. I'll see you again tomorrow."

Unperturbed, he replied, "Yes, I expect you shall. Have a very good evening."

Since Jeremiah was going to dispose of the room, there was nothing left to do except exit the place with as much dignity as possible. Nathan looped his free arm through Hannah's, then led her out into the corridor, and down the stairs to the lobby. Luckily, the clerk at the front desk was occupied with checking in a late arrival, an over-dressed woman with enough trunks piled around her to make it seem as though she was moving house rather than checking in to a hotel.

To Nathan's relief, Hannah remained silent until they were safely out of the hotel and standing near the curb, waiting to hail a cab. Her lips were pressed tightly together, as though that physical effort was the only thing that prevented her from speaking, but she kept quiet as they got into the cab he'd flagged down. Even once they were seated, she said nothing.

Beginning to be somewhat troubled by her silence, Nathan ventured, "It is best that we get this over with. It won't be easy, but—"

"That is not it!" she burst out at last. "Do you think I am afeared—*afraid,* I mean—of my fami-ly?" She paused there, and pulled in a breath in an attempt to calm herself. The way her accent had slipped out told him something of how upset she was, but he knew that to interrupt her now was the worst thing he could do. "It will be a blow to them, but they will manage. No, it was how your brother looked at me, as though I was some loose woman you had found on the street! We did nothing wrong! I am your *wife!*"

"I know," he said quietly, and took her hand in his. Her rage was such that he thought he could feel her actually shaking with it. He longed to pull her into his arms, kiss her, but he could tell she would not be receptive to such caresses. Not right now. Later, he would try to find a way to comfort her. "He is very angry with me. You see, he likes to think he has us all controlled. For me to go off and do something like this without his approval… it is not sitting well at all. He will calm down eventually, however."

"Oh, he seemed calm enough," Hannah retorted. "That is what worries me. It is the cold, calculating sort of anger that can be the very worst of all."

How could Nathan argue with such a statement? Hannah might have just met his brother, but it seemed she already had Jeremiah's measure. "Yes, that is true enough. But really, what can he do? We are married. It is all legal, completely aboveboard. He may be angry for a while, but as soon as he comes to really know you, he will understand that this is for the best."

"I hope you are right."

That was all she seemed inclined to say. Although she didn't take her hand from his, she sat there next to him with her slender body stiff with anger…or perhaps it was merely apprehension, worry over how their marriage would be received by her family.

Well, he was worried, too. But he had the marriage certificate safely tucked back in the breast pocket of his coat, and, like Jeremiah, the McAllisters would just have to come to terms with their new reality.

The cab stopped in front of the modest house on Stuyvesant Street. Nathan got out and paid the cabbie, then offered a hand to Hannah so she might have some help in alighting from the carriage. In the spare gaslight on the street, her face looked paler than usual.

But perhaps it wasn't the lighting at all.

"I am here," he murmured to her as they ascended the steps. "I'll always be here for you."

She offered him a grateful smile as she put her hand on the doorknob. Almost as soon as they entered the building, a swarm of people descended on them, both young and old, male and female, all talking at once in accents so thick, Nathan had a hard time understanding them.

Hannah raised her voice over all of them, calling out, "I am fine. Nothing is wrong. It's only —" She paused, teeth worrying at her lower lip, even as Nathan gave her an encouraging nod.

"Everyone, this is Nathan Wilcox. He's—he's my husband."

The babble abruptly halted. A tall man with graying sandy hair pushed himself to the front of the crowd and surveyed Nathan with a narrow-eyed glance before looking back over at Hannah. "Yer what?"

"My husband," she said distinctly, crossing her arms so the emerald and diamond band glittered on her finger. "We met, and fell in love. And today we got married. Nathan, show them."

All those watching eyes felt as if they were boring into him. Trying to ignore the onslaught, Nathan pulled the marriage license from his pocket and handed it to the man, who he guessed must be Hannah's Uncle Joseph.

A heavy silence as he perused the contents of the paper he held. Then he let out a heavy breath. "Ye have done it this time, haven't ye?"

"I've done nothing wrong," Hannah said. "I am a grown woman, free to make my own choices."

"But ye weren't so free, were ye? Or have ye forgotten that ye already had a betrothed?"

"One you chose for me," she shot back. She looked away from Joseph, toward a sandy-haired man probably closer to Hannah's age than Nathan's. "I am sorry, Boyd. But I know you'll find someone else."

Boyd's shoulders lifted. If he was angry or saddened by what Hannah had done, he showed no sign of it. However, there was no mistaking the brusqueness of his tone as he said, "Ye've dishonored the clan, that's what ye've done."

Before Hannah could make a reply, Nathan said, "I'm sorry to hear you feel that way. I know this has come as a shock to everyone, but certainly no dishonor was done here. Our marriage is a legal one. I love Hannah, and want to make her happy. Surely you can't wish her to be unhappy?"

Only another shrug from Boyd, who wouldn't meet Nathan's eyes. Joseph, still scowling, said, "Well, and it's clear enough ye're a smooth talker, Mr. Wilcox. So may I ask what ye plan now?"

"I brought Hannah home so she could tell all of you the news. There are still some…arrangements…I need to make with my own family, and so we thought it best for her to stay here tonight, get her belongings packed. Then I will return tomorrow morning and bring her home with me."

"And where will ye take her after that? Ye're none of the Van Horns, that I can tell."

"No," Nathan replied. "Like the McAllisters, the Wilcox clan is headed west. We may end up being neighbors in the Arizona Territories. So it is not as if you will never see Hannah again."

"Ach," said Joseph, which could have meant anything at all. He crossed his arms. "Then go and manage your 'business,' Mr. Wilcox, and we'll see that Hannah is ready for ye in the morning."

"Thank you, Mr. McAllister. I appreciate that." Nathan turned to Hannah. Her eyes were imploring—he could tell she wanted him to take her away with him now. And God, how he wished he could. First, though, he must settle things with Jennie. "It is only one night, my love," he told Hannah, his tone lowered. "I will be back in the morning, and then we will spend all the rest of our nights together."

"You swear," she said fiercely.

"Yes, I swear it. Nothing will keep me from your side, I promise." She gave a reluctant nod. He set down her valise, then said, "I will call at ten. I trust that will not be too early?"

"Ten will be sufficient."

There didn't seem to be anything more to say. He could not embrace Hannah passionately in front of all those witnesses—including her jilted fiancé—but he did bend down and place a gentle kiss on her cheek. "Only tonight," he whispered. "And then we'll be together."

He offered a nod to Joseph, and then turned and let himself out the front door. Shutting it behind him was one of the hardest things Nathan had ever done, but he forced himself to walk down the steps, to hail another cab, to go to the boarding house where Jennie waited.

As soon as he let himself in, she was waiting for him, dark eyes filled, not with rage, but with tears. Damn it. Jeremiah must have told her. The man always had to manage everything himself, even when he knew he should keep his nose out of other people's business.

"How could you?" she said, her voice shaking. "Nathan, how could you *do* such a thing?"

"Jennie—" He paused, all too aware of how they stood in the foyer, where anyone might overhear them. True, all the doors to his family members' rooms were currently shut, but that didn't mean they might not still be eavesdropping. Samuel in particular had a talent for listening at keyholes. "May we go speak in your room?"

She hesitated for a moment—he had never asked to enter her room before—but then nodded. "Perhaps that would be better."

He followed her into the chamber, a plain, cramped space with a dark, boxy dresser, an iron bedstead, and not much else. However, he noted a hand-painted vase sitting on the dresser, with one soft pink rose blooming within. That flower seemed just like Jennie, and another wave of guilt washed over him.

"Would you like to sit?" she asked him, her tone formal.

There was only one chair, a seat as plain and hard-edged as the rest of the furniture in the rented space. Nathan shook his head. "No, thank you. I—" He hesitated, knowing there was no way to say this gracefully. Well, he could only hope he might find some grace in the truth. "Jennie, I cannot varnish this and make it pretty. You are a good woman. You deserve happiness. But I don't believe you would have found it with me."

"Because you don't love me."

How could she sound so steady as she said such a thing? The tears he'd first glimpsed were still there, but he realized now she would never let them fall. He had to respect her quiet strength, even if she didn't inspire the same passion in him that Hannah did. "I care about you," he said. "But no, I do not love you. Not in the way that I love Hannah. And I have seen the example of my brother's marriage. I do not want to follow in those footsteps."

"You truly think I am like Lisbeth?"

Ah, so for all her outward patience, Jennie had no fondness for Jeremiah's wife, either. "No," he replied at once. "Not at all. But a marriage without love is a torment for all involved."

He could see the way her breast rose and fell as she took in a deep breath. One hand rose to touch the garnet brooch that glittered at her throat. "It would not have been a marriage without love," she said, her eyes meeting his. "At least, not on my side."

How could he reply to that? There might have been reproach in her eyes, but he heard none in her voice. "I am very sorry, Jennie."

"I'm sure you are." She stood quietly for a moment, then went on, "You do realize this puts me in a difficult position, don't you? My family washed their hands of me when I stayed with you, rather than denounce Jeremiah's experiments, his breaking with tradition to become *primus* of his own clan. I cannot think they will be so very happy to see me."

"I'm sorry," he said again, even though he knew the words were empty, useless. "I would rather believe that they will be relieved to see you come back to them. They will have a daughter returned, rather than a daughter lost."

"It is a pleasant fantasy, I suppose." Her chin lifted, and she added, "One way or another, I will find out soon enough."

"Jennie—" Nathan began, although he truly didn't know what he could say to offer any real comfort.

"Thank you, Nathan," she said. "I am rather tired. I think I wish to go to sleep now."

Which meant rather that she didn't wish to speak with him any further. Well, he could hardly blame her for that.

"Good night, Jennie," he said, and let himself out. For a moment, he lingered in the hallway, not because he thought she would come out to offer some parting barb, but because he wondered whether Jeremiah would appear and take him properly to task, now that the two of them were alone.

However, the *primus* did not emerge from his room, and after a moment, Nathan shrugged and went to his own bedchamber.

This would be the last night he had to sleep alone. A thrill went through him at the thought of having Hannah as his wife, all her fire and beauty and passion. Yes, Jeremiah was angry—and no doubt the rest of his family would take their cue from him—but in the end, they would all come to love Hannah as well, would realize her spirit was precisely what they needed in their new home.

Nathan was sure of that.

9

"I will take ye to the Wilcoxes' home," Uncle Joseph said, his tone not allowing for any possibility of an argument.

Hannah crossed her arms and glared up at him. "Nathan said he would come here to get me."

"No, they sent a messenger this morning, said something had come up and I was to bring ye. Are ye all packed, then?"

"Yes," she replied. This all sounded very suspicious, but perhaps they had had more difficulty with Nathan's former fiancée than expected, and therefore required some additional time to get the problem managed. At least her uncle was offering to take her to the Wilcoxes' flat. It wasn't as though he had vowed to never let her set foot outside again.

And she should also be grateful that she hadn't seen hide nor hair of Boyd this morning. He'd promptly disappeared the night before almost as soon as Nathan had left, hadn't offered her a single word, whether of condemnation or anger. Hannah didn't know whether she should be irritated or relieved by this behavior. On the one hand, it was good to have avoided an outright confrontation with him. On the other, he wasn't exactly behaving like a jilted fiancé.

Maybe he was just as relieved to be rid of her as she was of him.

"Then let us go," Joseph said, picking up her two valises and heading out the door.

Hannah allowed herself a mental shrug and followed him. It was also strange that none of her clan members were around to make their good-byes. Yes, they must be feeling betrayed right now, but still, family pride should have required them to give her a proper sendoff. Well, if that was how they wished to behave, so be it. The Wilcoxes would be her clan now anyway.

Her uncle would probably rather have been boiled in oil than waste money on a cab, and so they headed to the streetcar stop, and waited for the next car. Uncle Joseph seemed even more taciturn than usual, which suited Hannah. She would much rather daydream about her new life with Nathan than try to engage in stilted conversation

—especially if such conversation most likely would have included a few backhanded comments about her new husband. Better to think about waking up next to him every morning, to try to imagine their home in Arizona. Would there be mountains? Trees, or merely miles of desert? No matter. She didn't much care whether the Arizona Territories looked like the surface of the moon, as long as she was Nathan's wife.

The rented flat where the Wilcoxes were staying was much nicer than the one that currently housed the McAllister clan. Judging by the way Nathan and his brother Jeremiah dressed —and by the emerald and diamond band she now proudly wore on her left hand—the Wilcox family must be doing well for itself. Not that such petty concerns had entered her mind before this, since she knew she would have loved Nathan even if he had been penniless. Even so, it would be nice to not have to worry about money. She'd heard that some witch clans used their powers to increase their wealth, but that was not the McAllister way.

She supposed she'd find out soon enough whether it was the Wilcox way.

When Uncle Joseph knocked at the door of the flat, a very pretty woman with the same shining black hair and dark, dark eyes as Nathan and Jeremiah opened it. She smiled at Hannah, a welcoming, open smile.

"Good morning. I'm Mrs. Garnett—that is, Nathan's sister Emma. Please come in. They're expecting you."

"They"? Hannah could feel her eyebrows beginning to lift, but she smiled in return. "It is so good to meet you, Emma. This is my uncle, Joseph McAllister."

He offered a brusque hand for her to shake. "Pleased. Where do we need to go?"

"First door on the right, second floor," Emma replied. "You can leave those valises here for now."

Still feeling slightly puzzled, Hannah watched as Uncle Joseph set her cases on the floor, then went ahead and followed him up the stairs to the room her new sister-in-law had indicated. The door stood open, apparently as an invitation for them to enter without knocking.

As soon as she was inside, though, Hannah stopped dead. Sitting in a large chair in the center of the room was a woman she had never seen before, grey-haired and stern-faced, with the fine bones of someone who had probably been quite a beauty in her youth. She wore an intricate gown of ruffled black silk, with an enormous jet brooch glittering at her throat. At her side stood Jeremiah Wilcox. His dark eyes gleamed as he met Hannah's gaze, and he offered her a thin-lipped smile.

She could take no comfort from that smile,

however, because then she saw how Nathan was standing off to one side, flanked by a pair of men she did not know, but who were also dark-haired and dark-eyed. More brothers, she guessed, since the resemblance among all the family members was quite strong. A little ways away from them was someone she thought must be Emma's husband, for he was not quite as dark as the Wilcox brothers. From the way the two men stood, just slightly blocking Nathan, it seemed clear enough to her that they had done so in order to prevent him from moving forward to greet her.

"What on earth is going on?" she demanded. "Nathan?"

His eyes met hers in mute entreaty, but he did not speak.

The imposing woman in the black dress stood, her silken skirts rustling as she moved. "Hannah McAllister, you do not know me. I am Eugenia Van Horn."

Hearing that name spoken made Hannah's heart beat a little faster. No, she did not know Mrs. Van Horn personally, but of course she knew *of* her, knew that she was the *prima* of the clan that held sway here in New York. And she also knew that Mrs. Van Horn was probably not here on a social call, especially not with the way the woman's cold blue eyes studied her, no doubt taking in every defect of her dress and manner.

"Pleased to make your acquaintance, Mrs. Van Horn," she said.

"I doubt you will be so very pleased once you have heard what I have to say, but that is no matter." The Van Horn *prima* paused for a moment, her gaze considering. "However, I would like to congratulate you on your speech. You have done a very good job of erasing the Highlands from your voice. A natural ear, I suppose."

Quite a talent, to make a compliment sound like an insult. Hannah bristled, but she realized it would be foolish to call out the woman's comment. And one would think a remark like that would make Uncle Joseph speak up to defend his homeland, but he remained curiously silent. Indeed, from the way he was studiously not looking at her, and from the sick feeling that began to roil in her stomach, she started to suspect that he had been in on this from the beginning.

Whatever "this" was. As Mrs. Van Horn had just said, Hannah doubted she would like it very much.

"Clearly, you have something to say to me, Mrs. Van Horn. I would very much appreciate it if you would tell me, so I might go to speak with my husband."

"Ah, about that." She turned her head toward

the Wilcox *primus,* who had been silently watching this exchange. "Jeremiah, if you would."

He reached inside his black frock coat and produced a folded piece of paper. With dawning horror, Hannah looked on as he unfolded it and handed it to the *prima.* Even from this distance, Hannah knew immediately that it was her marriage license.

"What are you doing with that?" she cried out. "Nathan, why do they have our license?"

Her husband shook his head, eyes pleading with her to somehow understand. He began to make a gesture toward his mouth, but was stopped by one of his brothers, who took his arm and held it at his side.

"I'm afraid Mr. Wilcox can't speak with you right now," Mrs. Van Horn said. "One of my little talents. Very handy when raising six children, that much I can tell you. You see, the last thing I wanted was for him to interrupt me as I explained all this to you. This," she went on, taking the license and tearing it in half, then in half again, before flicking the paper with one aristocratic finger so it dissolved into ash before Hannah's horrified eyes, "was very badly done. Far be it from me to impugn the passions of youth, but you both made a very poor choice here. Perhaps you were innocent of the rules you were breaking, but ignorance of the law is never a defense. You see, this is *my* territory, the Van Horn clan's territory. Both the McAllister and the Wilcox clans are here on my sufferance, and with my permission. You—and Mr. Wilcox there—did not ask leave to break your engagements and marry one another while in Van Horn territory. Moreover, your rash decision caused harm and grief to your individual clans. Therefore, your marriage is null and void. Nathan Wilcox is not your husband. Members of my clan are already expediting the annulment, so your marriage will also have no standing in the nonmagical world."

"You can't do that!" Hannah burst out. She took a step forward, hands clenched, although she had no idea what she could possibly do to this formidable witch. But she could not stand there and allow such a terrible woman to destroy the only good and pure thing in her world.

"Oh, yes, I can," Eugenia Van Horn said calmly, even as Joseph reached out to take Hannah by the elbow and pull her back toward him. "I can, and I have. And by doing so, I am only doing what both your clan elders have asked of me. Mr. Jeremiah Wilcox most certainly did not want this marriage to continue, and neither did your Uncle Joseph, who appears to speak for your family."

"How *could* you?" Hannah rounded on her

uncle, tears of fury welling up in her eyes. "How could you hide this from me?"

"Ah, ye're a fine one to speak of 'hiding,' niece," Joseph responded, looking completely unruffled, despite the condemnation he must have heard in her voice. "Seems to me that ye were the one doing the sneaking around and hiding. But that's no nevermind. Boyd says he'll still have ye, and that's the important thing. Soon enough you'll forget this madness."

"I will never forget the man I love, not as long as I live." She turned away from her uncle and looked past Mrs. Van Horn to Nathan, who was now struggling openly to free himself from the two men who held him.

"Perhaps not," Jeremiah said. He glanced over at his brother, that thin, unpleasant smile returning to his lips. "But he will."

"What are you saying?" Even as she asked the question, Hannah feared the answer. After all, hadn't Nathan himself said that his brother Jeremiah was a man of many talents?

"I am saying, Miss McAllister, that by means of a simple spell, I can make Nathan forget about your very existence. Indeed, it is so effective that he will be able to walk past you on the street and not bat an eyelash, for you will be a perfect stranger to him."

"Ach, that's a terrible magic," Joseph blurted out, looking shocked despite himself.

"'Terrible'?" Jeremiah repeated. "I don't think so. Far worse for him to live out his days always thinking of what might have been. No, he will go away from here, and he will marry his fiancée Jennie—with the assistance of Mrs. Van Horn here—and he will lead a happy life."

"And what about me?" Hannah whispered.

"You?" A lift of the broad shoulders under the black frock coat. "Why, I suppose that depends on you, Miss McAllister. I have long believed that we all make our own happiness. You can either accept your lot in life, or you can bemoan what fate took away from you. Unless," he added, looking thoughtful, "you would prefer for me to cast that same spell on you? That way, you could also continue in blissful oblivion."

"No," she said at once. How could she voluntarily give up her memories of Nathan, of the few glorious hours she had spent in his arms? Better to at least know what perfect happiness could be, even if it would be forever denied her.

"Let the girl be a martyr if she wishes," Mrs. Van Horn said. "It does not matter to me, and it should not matter to you, Mr. Wilcox. Your fates are no longer entwined. But I have an engagement at noon, so if I am not needed here any longer—"

Jeremiah gave a small bow. "You have been of

great service to my clan, Mrs. Van Horn. Please, do not let us delay you any further. If you ever happen to travel out west, we will be at your service as well."

"'Out west'?" she repeated, and looked at the Wilcox *primus* blankly, as though he had just suggested she might fly to the moon. "Whyever would I want to visit such a place?"

"Just a fancy, Mrs. Van Horn."

She shook her head, then sailed toward the door, causing Joseph to pull Hannah out of the way. She had the notion to reach out and grab the Van Horn witch by the hair, stomp on the train of her dress—anything that might delay her, might give Hannah the opportunity to plead her case once more. But with her uncle's iron grip on her arm, she knew she could do nothing. Besides, how could her puny talents possibly prevail against the *prima* of one of America's oldest witch clans?

"I think our business here is concluded," Jeremiah said. "Unless, of course, you wish to stay and watch me cast the spell."

"Ye're an evil, evil man," Hannah spat at him. "And I hope ye burn in the fires of hell."

"Careful, Miss McAllister—your accent is slipping." Jeremiah Wilcox paused there for a moment, as if to consider her words. When she had first caught sight of him, back in the hotel room at the Astoria, she had thought him quite handsome, although in a forbidding way, not nearly as approachable as his youngest brother. Now, though, he looked like the very Devil himself. "As for the rest, well, I would beg to differ. I am only doing what I must to protect my clan. Jennie will make a worthy wife for him, and her skills are of far greater use to us than yours, for my sister is also a healer, and we have no need of another. We are a new clan, and are traveling to a rough part of the world. I cannot allow any room for sentimentality in that world." He stopped again, now with an almost pitying look in his coal-black eyes. "You are very young. You will survive this."

"If you had a heart of your own, you would not say such things."

He went very still then. "Oh, I do, Miss McAllister. I do. But I do not allow it to rule my life." His gaze moved from her to Joseph, who still held her by the arm. "I think it perhaps best that you take her from here now. And I would suggest that you make arrangements to leave New York as soon as possible. Mrs. Van Horn is not known for her patience."

"Ach, I can see that," Uncle Joseph replied. "Come along, my dear. Good thing that ye are already packed, for 'twill make things go faster."

No, this couldn't be happening. Surely she must be caught in a terrible dream, one she would wake from any moment now, to find the sun shining and the birds singing, and her husband waiting for her, ready to bring her into his life. But no, here was her uncle pulling her from the room, even as Nathan somehow managed to break free from the men who restrained him, darling Nathan who rushed across the chamber to seize her other arm, to bring her to him so he could give her one last despairing kiss.

"You force my hand," said Jeremiah. His black eyes glittered, and he muttered something under his breath.

What those syllables actually were, Hannah would never know. However, she could not help but witness their effect—the way Nathan suddenly let go of her and backed away, expression shocked and bewildered…and also blank, as though a stranger now stared at her where her lover had once been.

"I—I beg your pardon, miss. I don't know what I was thinking—"

"Nathan!" she cried. "It's Hannah! I'm your wife. Please try to remember!"

"'Wife'?" he repeated, shaking his head. "No, I have no wife. I will soon, though—my intended's name is Jennie."

Oh, Goddess, this couldn't be happening. She tried to reach out to him again, but this time Uncle Joseph had his arm around her waist, was hastening her away. And she, now nearly blinded by tears, couldn't fight back. It was impossible. She couldn't fight them all.

Just before he hurried her down the stairs, she noticed a young dark-haired woman standing outside one of the doorways of the second-floor flat. She was very pretty, with her smooth oval face and large dark eyes. At once Hannah guessed who it must be. Jennie Winfield, Nathan's fiancée.

Oddly, though, the other woman's expression wasn't one of triumph. Instead, she gazed at Hannah with sadness in her eyes, and mouthed two words.

I'm sorry.

That was all Hannah could see, for then the tears truly did blind her, and she let her uncle lead her outside—after retrieving her two valises—and into a waiting cab. Jeremiah Wilcox must have paid for it. No doubt he didn't want anything to interfere with her hasty removal.

She leaned her head against the window and wept, hating Jeremiah, hating her uncle, hating Mrs. Van Horn. Indeed, she was filled with so much hate, she didn't know if her heart would ever hold anything else.

And in that moment, she simply didn't care.

Her world had ended.

EPILOGUE

THE MCALLISTERS SETTLED IN JEROME, AS they had planned. And when the Wilcoxes came west, they arrived in Flagstaff and decided to go no further. This was mainly Jeremiah's decision, for as *primus* he had the final say. When asked what had made him linger there and not continue on to the shining promise of California, he would always reply that he loved the mountains, and knew this was where his clan was meant to stay. Sometimes, though, his gaze would slide to the southwest, and he would smile slightly, as though at a secret amusement.

In the depths of winter, just before the turn of the year, Boyd and Hannah McAllister welcomed a boy. The child's hair and eyes were black as coal, exceedingly strange in a baby born to parents with reddish hair and light-colored eyes. He bore no resemblance to either of them, or to the brothers and sisters who would follow in the years to come.

And yet, everyone in the clan knew better than to comment on this apparent oddity, just as they made sure never to have anything to do with the Wilcox family, even though they were almost neighbors. The years passed, and as tragedy after tragedy was visited upon the heirs of Jeremiah's line, the McAllisters could not help but feel a certain inner satisfaction. Evil doings led to evil outcomes, after all.

Until, many, many years later, Hannah's great-great-great-great-granddaughter gave birth to a child she named Angela....

The End

The modern-day storyline of the Witches of Cleopatra Hill will continue in *Deep Magic* (October 2017) and conclude in *Darktide*, due out in January 2018.

THE ARIZONA WITCH CLANS

The McAllisters (Jerome, Arizona, and the Verde Valley)

Angela McAllister (Wilcox) – *prima*, or head witch, of the McAllister clan

Rachel McAllister – Angela's aunt

Bryce McAllister – one of the McAllister clan's elders

Allegra Moss – one of the McAllister clan's elders

Margot Emory (Wilcox) – formerly one of the McAllister clan's elders, now married to Lucas Wilcox

Sylvia Emory – Margot's mother

Ruby Lynch – former *prima* of the McAllister clan

Henry Lynch – son of Ruby McAllister and Patrick Lynch

Tobias Miller – fiancé of Rachel McAllister

Sonya McAllister – Angela's mother, deceased

Boyd Willis – a McAllister warlock

Micah Landon -- an absentminded artist

Floyd Barnett – lives above the store next to Rachel's

Rosemary McAllister – lives on the other side of Rachel's store above the tea shop

Susan Callery -- an artist with a studio in the same building as Tobias' flat

Efraim Willendale -- runs the post office

Wyatt McAllister -- owns a B&B on Paradise Street

Dora McAllister – Great-Aunt Ruby's caretaker

Jocelyn Riggs -- the clan's strongest medium

Kirby McAllister – a cousin of Angela's and one of her "caretakers"

Tricia McAllister -- the new clan elder after Margot Emory steps down

Richard McAllister – Tricia's husband

Caitlin McAllister (Trujillo) – daughter of Tricia and Richard; a seer

Michael McAllister – Caitlin's older brother, a chef

Roslyn McAllister -- Caitlin's first cousin; youngest sister of Jenny and Adam

Marcus McAllister -- Tricia McAllister's older brother, father of Jenny, Adam, and Roslyn

Lysette McAllister – Marcus' wife and mother of Jenny, Adam, and Roslyn; a civilian (non-witch)

Jenny McAllister – eldest daughter of Marcus and Lysette McAllister

Adam McAllister – only son of Marcus and Lysette McAllister

Roslyn McAllister – youngest daughter of Marcus and Lysette McAllister

Evan McAllister—a distant cousin of Angela's; the clan's "fixer"

The Wilcox Clan (Flagstaff, Arizona, and the northern third of the state)

Connor Wilcox – *primus* (head warlock) of the Wilcox clan

Damon Wilcox – former *primus* of the Wilcoxes, now deceased

Lucas Wilcox – a cousin of Connor's, now married to Margot Emory

Mason Wilcox (McAllister) – Connor's cousin and a friend of Angela's; now married to Adam McAllister

Danica Wilcox – Mason's younger sister

Joseph Wilcox – Mason and Danica's father

Olivia Wilcox – Mason and Danica's mother

Andre Begonie – Angela McAllister's father

Marie Wilcox (Begonie) – a cousin of Connor's, the Wilcox clan's seer

Eleanor Garnett – the clan's healer

Darrell Wilcox – a Wilcox warlock gifted with heating the area around him

In the 1880s:

Jeremiah Wilcox – the Wilcox clan's *primus*

Nizhoni – Jeremiah's second wife, a woman of the Navajo

Jacob Wilcox – Jeremiah and Nizhoni's son

Samuel Wilcox – Jeremiah's brother

Edmund Wilcox – Jeremiah's brother

Nathan Wilcox – Jeremiah's brother

Emma Garnett – Jeremiah's only sister; children are Louis, Susan, Marcus, and Jeffrey

Aaron Garnett – Emma's husband

Grace Wilcox – Samuel's wife; five children are Benjamin, Addie, Esther, Clay, and Dorothy

Lida Wilcox – Edmund's wife; their three children are Kathleen, Annabelle, and Wyatt

Jennie Wilcox – Nathan's wife; their four children are Oliver, Calvin, Levi, and Victor

The de la Paz clan (Phoenix, Arizona; Tucson, Arizona; and the southern third of the state)

Maya de la Paz -- *prima* of the de la Paz clan up through *Protector*

Alex Trujillo -- Maya's grandson

Diego Trujillo -- Alex's older brother

Alicia Trujillo – Alex and Diego's little sister

Letty Trujillo – Diego's wife

Luz Trujillo – Alex and Diego's mother and Maya's daughter; *prima* of the de la Paz clan after the end of *Protector*

David Trujillo – Luz's husband and father of Alex, Diego, and Alicia

Valentina de la Paz – the de la Paz clan's healer in the Tucson area

Alba de la Paz -- the healer in the Phoenix area

Zoe Sandoval – the de la Paz clan's *prima*-in-waiting

Zander Sandoval – Zoe's little brother

Luis Sandoval – father of Zoe and Zander

Andrea Sandoval – mother of Zoe and Zander, Alex Trujillo's aunt (Luz and Andrea are sisters)

Luis de la Paz – Alex's cousin; works at the family's store

Jack Sandoval -- Luis Sandoval's youngest brother; a detective with the Scottsdale P.D.

Miguel de la Paz -- a private detective

Oscar de la Paz -- with the Tucson P.D.

Defender

Bad Blood

Deep Magic (October 2017)

Dark tide (January 2018)

THE DJINN WARS

(Paranormal Romance)

Chosen

Taken

Fallen

Broken

Forsaken

Forbidden

Awoken

Illuminated (December 2017)

THE SEDONA FILES

(Paranormal Romance)

Bad Vibrations

Desert Hearts

Angel Fire

Star Crossed

Falling Angels

Enemy Mine

TALES OF THE LATTER KINGDOMS

(Fantasy Romance)

All Fall Down

Dragon Rose

Binding Spell

Ashes of Roses

One Thousand Nights

Threads of Gold

The Wolf of Harrow Hall

Moon Dance

The Song of the Thrush (November 2017)

THE GAIAN CONSORTIUM SERIES

(Science Fiction Romance)

Blood Will Tell

ABOUT THE AUTHOR

Christine Pope has been writing stories ever since she commandeered her family's Smith-Corona typewriter back in the sixth grade. Her work includes paranormal romance, fantasy romance, and science fiction/space opera romance. The Land of Enchantment cast its spell on her while she was researching her Djinn Wars series, and she now makes her home in Santa Fe, New Mexico.

To be notified about new releases by Christine Pope, please go to www.christinepope.com and sign up for her newsletter.